Emily Harvale lives ˙ [barcode] ˌ UK
– although she v ˌn the
French Alps ... or ˌ ˌere that
has several months ˌily loves
snow almost as much as ˌ ˌ Christmas.

Having worked in the ᴜ (London) for several years, Emily returned to her home town of Hastings where she spends her days writing ... and wondering if it will ever snow.

You can contact her via her website, Facebook or Instagram.

There is also a Facebook group where fans can chat with Emily about her books, her writing day and life in general. Details can be found on Emily's website.

Author contacts:
www.emilyharvale.com
www.twitter.com/emilyharvale
www.facebook.com/emilyharvalewriter
www.instagram.com/emilyharvale

\*\*\*

Scan the code above to see all Emily's books on Amazon

Part Four – Trick or treat
Christmas on Lily Pond Lane
Return to Lily Pond Lane
A Wedding on Lily Pond Lane
Secret Wishes and Summer Kisses on Lily Pond Lane

## Wyntersleap series
Christmas at Wynter House – Book 1
New Beginnings at Wynter House – Book 2
A Wedding at Wynter House – Book 3
Love is in the Air – spin off

## Merriment Bay series
Coming Home to Merriment Bay – Book 1
(four-part serial)
Part One – A Reunion
Part Two – Sparks Fly
Part Three – Christmas
Part Four – Starry Skies
Chasing Moonbeams in Merriment Bay – Book 2
Wedding Bells in Merriment Bay – Book 3

## Seahorse Harbour series
Summer at my Sister's – book 1
Christmas at Aunt Elsie's – book 2
Just for Christmas – book 3
Tasty Treats at Seahorse Bites Café – book 4
Dreams and Schemes at The Seahorse Inn – book 5
Weddings and Reunions in Seahorse Harbour – book 6

## Clementine Cove series
Christmas at Clementine Cove – book 1
Broken Hearts and Fresh Starts at Cove Café – book 2
Friendships Blossom in Clementine Cove – book 3

## Norman Landing series
Saving Christmas – book 1
A not so secret Winter Wedding – book 2
Sunsets and surprises at Seascape Café-book 3
A Date at the end of The Pier – book 4

**Locke Isle series**
A Summer Escape – book 1
Christmas on Locke Isle – book 2

**Betancourt Bay series**
That Mistletoe Moment – book 1
That Winter Night – book 2
That Special Something – book 3

ISBN 978-1-909917-99-6

Published by Crescent Gate Publishing

Print edition published worldwide 2024
E-edition published worldwide 2024

Cover design by JR and Emily Harvale

# Acknowledgements

My grateful thanks go to the following:

My webmaster, David Cleworth who does so much more than website stuff.
My cover design team, JR.
Luke Brabants. Luke is a talented artist and can be found at: www.lukebrabants.com
My wonderful friends for their friendship and love. You know I love you all.
All the fabulous members of my Readers' Club. You help and support me in so many ways and I am truly grateful for your ongoing friendship. I wouldn't be where I am today without you.
My Twitter and Facebook friends, and fans of my Facebook author page. It's great to chat with you. You help to keep me (relatively) sane!

To Florence and Jonty.
The best author assistants in the world
… even if you are cats.
Without your constant purrs in my ears,
and edits to my manuscripts when you
walk across my keyboard,
my life wouldn't be half as much fun.
Is fun the word I'm looking for?
Hand me that thesaurus. xxx

# Emily Harvale

# That Special Something

CRESCENT GATE PUBLISHING

# MAP KEY – BETANCOURT BAY

1) **Lookout Point** – At **310 feet**, this is the highest point on the white cliffs around Betancourt Bay. You can see Locke Isle from here while seated on the bench, and on a very clear day, even the coast of France. **Lookout Steps** lead down to the sandy beach – but there are **300 steps**, so most people access the beach farther along, where the cliff paths aren't so steep and there are fewer steps.

2) **Sunnycliff Cottage - James and Margaret Hart** live here. They have two daughters, **Fiona** and **Naomi**. Fiona lives in Folkestone with her boyfriend. Naomi is single and lives in Lewisham (London) where she rents a flat with two friends.

3) **Willow Cottage** – Home to **Malorie Blackwell**, a reflexologist.

4) **Seaview Cottage** – **Laurence Lake** lives here. He's a successful author of several cosy crime books.

5) **Rosehip Cottage** – **Jean and**

**Victor Mills** live here. Their four children, **Tom, Rob, Zoe and Tara** have all moved away but they come home for high days and holidays.

6) **Betancourt** – Ancestral home to the Betancourt family which currently consists of **Archie Betancourt**, his second wife, **Bianca** (his first wife **Francesca**, died) and his two sons, **Grifforde (known as Griff)** and **Russell.**

7) **Mr and Mrs Bernard and Barbra Brimble's B & B** – **Barbra** describes herself as 'a people person'; people describe her as 'a nosy gossip' – but not to her face. She loves to sing, and often does, whether others want her to or not.

8) **Clifftop Farm** – Once part of the Betancourt's estate, but now a small holding owned by **Sandy and Sonia Grey**, most of the farmland having been sold-off by various Betancourts over the years. Sandy and Sonia are known for taking in all sorts of waifs and strays, both human and animal.

9) **The Royal Oak** pub – Although highly unlikely, legend has it that King Richard (The Lionheart) once sat beneath the ancient oak tree opposite the pub, on his way to join the Crusades. Owned and run by **Freddie Tollard** and his daughter, **Charlotte (Charlie)**

10) **The White House** – Home to **Simon and Patience (Pat) Eversley** and daughters **Grace** and **Hope** along with their dog, **Lady Elizabeth, known as Lady E**. The Eversleys run an Events company, **Eversley Events** from here.

11) The Rectory – **The Reverend Brian Copeland** and his wife **Daisy** live here.

12) **St Gabriel's Church** – with a bijou village hall attached. The church was built in 1086, the hall in 1946.

13) **Catkin Cottage** – Home to **Hanna Shaw**, an artist.

14) **Acorn Cottage** – Elderly sisters, **Rita and Vera Boot** have lived here all their lives.

15) **Bluebell Cottage – Greg Bishop** lives here. He owns a bookshop in Folkestone.

16) **Oak View Cottage – Molly Law** has recently inherited this cottage from her grandmother, **Millicent**. Molly lives in Folkestone with her parents, **Owen and Nikki**.

17) **Betancourt Bay Café** – Owned by **Derek Dunpole** and his (miserable) wife, **Doris**, who had much grander plans than running a café in a small village, as she constantly reminds her long-suffering husband.

18) **West Wood** – owned by the Betancourts but they allow the villagers to use it.

19) **East Wood** – also owned by the Betancourts, who allow the villagers access.

**Wish you were here?**

This new series is set in Betancourt Bay, a fictional, clifftop village a mile from Folkestone. I've, sort of, 'demolished' everything that currently occupies this space in real life, and 'built' Betancourt Bay there instead. Apologies for that, but it was a necessary evil in order for me to tell these stories.

In addition to this, I have added a few fictional things/places/businesses in Folkestone – like the slipway where the Locke Isle Ferry docks, among others, so please forgive me for that!

This series also links to my other new series, Locke Isle, which is set on the fictional island of Locke Isle, two miles off the Kent coast, and also partly in the real town of Folkestone.

So if you know Folkestone and the surrounding area, you may not entirely recognise it when you read these books...

With love,
Emily xx

# One

'You're late.'

Hope tapped her watch and tutted good naturedly as her elder sister dashed into the cosy kitchen of The White House for the Sunday morning meeting of Eversley Events, the events planning company set up by Pat and Simon Eversley fifteen years before. Grace had joined the business straight from school; Hope, on the other hand, couldn't wait to go to university but she returned once she had gained her degree, and joined the, by then, already thriving family enterprise.

'I know,' said Grace, puffing out her red cheeks and huffing out a sigh of exhaustion. 'But with good reason. You won't believe what's happened.'

'You haven't been mugged, have you?' Hope was joking. But not entirely.

'No. But I do have news about that.' Grace looked pleased with herself as her tone rose an octave or two. She joined her family at the large, circular, pine kitchen table and dropped on to an empty chair.

Although not all the Eversley family sat around the table. Pat's mum, Granny Joy, was snoring softly in the armchair situated between the inglenook fireplace where a log fire roared, and the big green Aga in which Sunday lunch was cooking, having joked that she wanted to get nice and toasty on both sides. Lady Elizabeth, the family's French Bulldog known as Lady E, was fast asleep in her comfy basket next to the Aga, one small paw resting on her water bowl beside her.

Mingled with the smell of beef slowly roasting in the oven of the fairly ancient Aga, the aroma of coffee permeated the air as it always did between the hours of seven a.m. and noon in the Eversley household, and Hope poured her sister a cup from the pot on the table without enquiring if Grace wanted one.

'News about Naomi's mugging?' Pat, their mum, queried.

'Have the police finally done their job and found the culprit?' asked Simon, their dad.

Grace took a sip of coffee, eyeing her family over the rim of the cup while raising the forefinger of her free hand.

'I needed that,' she said, letting out another sigh.

'Are you going to keep us in suspense all morning?' Hope said.

Grace took another sip and then shook her head. 'I'm not sure where to start.'

'Who cares,' said Hope. 'But start at the best bit. You can add the details later.'

'There're two best bits,' said Grace, now barely able to contain her obvious excitement. 'Naomi's handsome stranger has reappeared. He was outside the café yesterday, looking for her. She saw him while out on a walk. His name is Lucas Dove and he says he feels the same way about her as she feels about him. They went for a drink at The Royal Oak and now they're dating! It turns out he had only recently moved to Folkestone and had got lost the day they first met. Isn't that incredible? It's clearly Fate. I mean what are the chances?'

'Blimey!' Hope glanced around at the others who were all as equally astonished.

Naomi Hart, who was the older sister of Hope's best friend Fiona, had met a handsome stranger in Betancourt Bay Café two weeks before, having been mugged after her car had broken down a mile or two outside the village. She had gone to the café for help because her handbag, containing her mobile phone, had been stolen and she wanted to call her family and the police. The café was the closest place on a cold and snowy January night. The owners of the café, Doris and Derek Dunpole had been their usual unfriendly selves, but the handsome stranger had lent her his phone and bought her a hot chocolate. A commotion had then ensued between the Dunpoles and in the confusion, Naomi and the stranger had parted ways without exchanging names or numbers.

But that winter night hadn't been all bad for Naomi. Not only did she meet the man of her dreams, she also found a two-pound coin on the pavement and bought a Lottery ticket with it the following Wednesday. No one was more amazed than Naomi to discover she had won the sum of one million two hundred and fifty-one thousand nine-hundred and forty-five pounds and thirty-two pence, which was in her bank account less than a week after a visit from a member of the Lottery team.

She immediately made an offer to buy Betancourt Bay Café and the sale was proceeding quickly. And now it seemed, she'd also got the man she had been searching for. "Blimey" didn't really cover it.

'Good heavens,' said Pat. 'And until recently, Naomi didn't seem to have much luck, did she? I'm so thrilled for her. Now all her dreams have come true. Isn't it strange how one's life can change so fast?'

'None of us know what it has in store for us,' said Simon, shaking his head as if he couldn't quite believe this news.

'Anyway,' Grace said, clearly eager to continue. 'Naomi called me this morning to tell me all about yesterday and I asked her round for coffee because Griff was in a meeting with Sandy and Sonia Grey. I assumed it was just something about Clifftop Farm they wanted to discuss with him, but it turned out it wasn't. Well, not exactly.'

Grace and Naomi, like Hope and Fiona, had been best friends growing up in Betancourt Bay, but Naomi had moved to London and they'd drifted apart somewhat, although they still met up sometimes when Naomi came home to visit her family.

And then Naomi had been made redundant from her position as manager of an Art Café, on top of which the rent on the flat she shared increased beyond her means. She had no other choice but to ask her parents if she could move back home temporarily and was planning to do so the weekend she was mugged.

Returning to Betancourt Bay meant Naomi's friendship with Grace had blossomed once again, and her life had gone from rock bottom on that first fateful night, to the mountain top in the space of a couple of weeks.

But in a way, so had Grace's. She had believed herself to be in love with Russell Betancourt for most of her life, although that love was unrequited.

Russell was the blond haired, blue eyed youngest son of Archie and Francesca, but Francesca sadly died more than twenty years ago and three and a half years later, Archie met, and soon after married, his second wife, Bianca. The Betancourts no longer owned the village nor the huge estate their ancestors had, but they were still a rich and powerful family, loved and respected by all who lived in Betancourt Bay and beyond. Although that love and respect did not extend to Bianca who did all she could to create a distance between the Betancourts and the villagers.

Then last Christmas the Eversleys had been hired by Griff Betancourt, Russell's older brother, to organise the annual Mistletoe Dance, the most prestigious event of the year which had been held at Betancourt for centuries. It had proved to be a revelation.

To her astonishment, Grace discovered it was Griff she was in love with, and as family secrets had been revealed, so had the fact that Griff had been in love with Grace for as long as she had believed herself to be in love with Russell.

The only small fly in the ointment, was

Russell. He had also declared his love that night – but not for Grace. For Hope.

Hope loved Russell dearly but only as a friend and when he had told her how he felt she had to let him down. She tried to do it gently. She even said she knew he was only teasing so she wasn't taking it seriously, hoping that such a comment might save him some embarrassment.

He seemed to realise her intention and he'd managed to laugh and make light of it, but they both knew the truth.

And so did most of the village it seemed because since Christmas Eve, not only her own family but almost all the residents of Betancourt Bay had been constantly telling her how wonderful Russell was, what a catch he would be, and how he'd make her blissfully happy.

Hope simply couldn't see it.

'Don't keep telling me how wonderful he is,' she snapped at her family shortly after the New Year. 'I know he's wonderful and kind and generous. I know he's handsome with his golden blond hair and blue eyes. I know he's rich and works for the family's auction house. I know that I'm insane not to bite his hand off and marry him immediately. But I can't. I don't know what it is but it's ... oh, I don't know ... there's simply something missing. I'm just not crazy about him. No bolts of electricity shoot through me when I look at him, or when he smiles at me, or touches my arm, or anything. And there should be, shouldn't there? Shouldn't I feel ... that special something when he's near me? Because I don't. And I can't pretend I do.'

After that, her family had been less forceful.

'Perhaps you'll grow to love him,' Grace had said hopefully.

'I've known him since I was about five,' Hope replied. 'I'm thirty now, so at this rate, I'll be about ninety-five when I fall in love with him. Just accept that it's not meant to be. Even Russell has.'

Hope was fairly sure he hadn't accepted anything of the sort, but he had told her he had and confirmed that they could just be friends. The problem was, he kept popping up wherever she was and now if she spotted him before he saw her, she had taken to hiding from him. Sometimes in the unlikeliest of places.

That wasn't easy, given the fact that the ornate iron gates of Betancourt were just across the road, and visible from the sitting room of The White House. The sweeping curved drive leading to the front door of the impressive but understated frontage of the stately home was a good half a mile long though with wide green lawns either side of the drive, and thankfully, between the gates and the house were rows of shrubs and trees lining the walls surrounding the estate, that blocked out a direct view of the ground floor rooms of both houses.

And luckily for Hope, there was a row of large evergreen Bay trees that hid the upstairs windows of The White House from the upstairs windows of Betancourt, no matter the angle you might try to view the cottage from, or which room you were in within the stately home. Hope had recently, and surreptitiously, checked. The last thing she needed was Russell Betancourt spying on her in her bedroom, from his.

Not that she thought he would. Russell wasn't a creep. Yet he did seem to have the uncanny ability to be wherever she was more often than not. Perhaps it was coincidence. They did have several friends and acquaintances in common. Even so, it was somewhat irksome at times.

But at least the close proximity of their homes was handy for Grace who now spent most of her nights at Betancourt. Grace and Griff had been together since the night of the Mistletoe Dance, and were head over heels in love. So much so that Grace was thinking of proposing.

'Well it is a leap year this year and women can propose on leap years,' Grace had stated only a few days ago.

Hope had pulled a face and rolled her eyes. 'We can propose whenever we want, Grace. We don't have to wait for a leap year. This is the twenty-first century, you know.' And then, realising the last thing she wanted right now was for her sister to propose to Griff, had hastily added, 'But just because we can, it doesn't mean we should.'

'What? Why not? He's asked me to move in with him.'

'Asking someone to live with you doesn't mean you're sure you want to marry them. That's the whole point of living with someone. You have all the benefits of marriage – apart from the tax breaks – but you also have the freedom to leave, or ask them to leave in Griff's case, anytime you want without having to deal with all the legal formalities of a divorce.'

Grace looked like one of the deflated balloons at the end of the engagement party bash at which they'd had this conversation.

'Are you saying that Griff's not sure he wants to spend the rest of his life with me? He told me himself that he does.'

Hope didn't want to upset Grace but she had an ulterior motive. 'People say all sorts of things when they're in love. And I'm sure it's true. But you've only been dating since Christmas and it's not even Valentine's Day yet. And please, please, please, don't tell me you're thinking of proposing on Valentine's Day.'

'What's wrong with that?' Grace said sheepishly.

'Grace! It's corny. It's boring. It's … just don't do it. Okay?'

Grace had shrugged. 'We might not have been dating that long but we've known one another for most of our lives. He's the one for me, Hope, and he says I'm the one for him. He's loved me most of his life, so why would he have doubts now?'

'I'm not saying he has doubts. I'm just suggesting you wait.'

'For what? For how long? Your problem is you've only been in love once and because that ended badly you think all relationships will.'

Hope had bristled at that. 'No I don't. I couldn't do this job and organise all the engagement parties, weddings, christenings etc if I did. But some do, you know. I'm not saying yours will. You and Griff were made for one another and I don't know why it took all of us so long to see it when it was so obvious last Christmas. All I'm saying is wait a bit longer. Besides, we can't fit in another surprise proposal or an engagement party. If you must do it, at least wait until March. From a purely practical viewpoint, we might not be quite so busy by then. I know we have at least two days in the diary free next month. Although since the Mistletoe Dance, we've been inundated, so that might be a moot point.'

The newly engaged couple had interrupted them at that precise moment to thank them for organising such a splendid party so nothing further was said about it that night, and in the days since, Grace hadn't mentioned it again.

Hope prayed she had dodged a bullet.

'What do you mean by "not exactly"?' Hope now asked Grace. 'Clifftop Farm is no longer part of the Betancourt's estate and hasn't been for years, so why would Sandy and Sonia need to discuss anything about their small holding with Griff?'

'Perhaps someone has complained about all the waifs and strays the couple take in,' suggested Pat, 'and they wanted to ask Griff to put in a good word. I know he's not the Lord and Master, although Archie has as good as passed the baton on to him, and the Betancourts don't own the village these days, but everyone still looks up to the Betancourts. Especially to Griff. If he told people to leave the Greys to get on with things, everyone would.'

Clifftop Farm had once been massive and owned by the Betancourts who rented it out to tenant farmers for centuries. Over the years land was sold off and a smaller area of farmland was sold to Mr and Mrs Bean who had both passed away when Hope was in her late teens. Even more of the land had been sold off since then and now Clifftop Farm was just a small holding with a few acres of land.

Sandy and Sonia Grey had moved there shortly after and they kept some sheep and other animals, but they were known as good Samaritans by the rest of the village as they often took in all sorts of waifs and strays, both animal and human. No one ever knew what or whom they might find in the Grey's cosy kitchen when they popped in for a cup of tea, or to see the lambs in the spring and help with feeding. But as far as Hope was aware, no one had ever complained about them.

Grace shook her head. 'That wasn't it. It wasn't about the farm or the animals. It was about someone they've taken in.' Her eyes lit up with excitement. 'It was also about Naomi's mugger.'

'What?' Hope shrieked. 'Are you seriously going to tell us that the man who mugged Naomi is staying at Clifftop Farm?'

Grace laughed. 'Nope. Because it wasn't a man. It was a young girl of twelve who Sandy and Sonia are fostering temporarily.

She said that it was the first time she had done anything like that but she'd been surrounded by gangs where she had lived in London and they'd often tried to persuade her to – in her own words, "steal and do other stuff like that", so she thought she'd give it a go. She'd only arrived at the farm on that Friday morning, and was feeling lost and lonely, apparently, so she'd stolen Sandy's bicycle and run away. But it was bitterly cold and she had no idea where to go so when she spotted Naomi, who had just fallen over and was getting back on her feet, the girl stole the bag hoping there would be money to buy a train ticket to London. The purse only had a few coins in it, and then she realised what she'd done and that the police might start looking for her, so she hurried back to the farm and was going to run away as soon as she could steal some money from Sandy or Sonia.'

'Good heavens!' Pat exclaimed. 'So how did Sandy and Sonia find out? Did they find Naomi's bag and purse?'

Grace shook her head. 'The girl came clean. To quote what she told us this morning, if I can remember the exact words, "They were really kind and the farmhouse was very warm and cosy and it was freezing outside. Plus the cops were probably looking for me, so I thought I'd stay the night. And then I liked it. The animals are so cool and I had a bedroom of my own. And a radiator in my room. I wanted to stay, but I knew I'd done something bad. I don't know why but I just blurted it out when we were watching *Midsomer Murders* on TV last night." That's almost word for word, I think. Obviously, everyone in the village, including Sandy and Sonia, had been talking about the mugging and saying what a nasty piece of work the mugger was and that they hoped Karma would pay the evil person back. And then when Naomi won the Lottery, everyone was saying that her win was the universe putting things right. The youngster did some thinking and decided that crime doesn't pay, and that if she did something good, she might be rewarded by the universe.'

'Ah. So she's hoping Naomi will give her some cash from the Lottery winnings, is she?' Simon said, looking cross. 'I doubt that very much. I hope Griff called the police.'

'No,' said Grace. 'The girl just wants to stay with Sandy and Sonia. She says she's really sorry and that she'll do whatever it takes to put things right. Griff called us in, when he realised Naomi was with me, and the girl repeated what she'd told Griff, and gave Naomi back her handbag, purse, and phone. Everything was there. So Naomi said she wouldn't report her if she swore never to do anything like it again. And then Sandy and Sonia suggested the youngster could help Naomi with cleaning the café and the flat above, once the sale completes, in lieu of community service, which is the most the girl would get if the police were involved. In fact, they'd probably let her off with a caution.'

'Was the girl genuinely sorry?' Hope asked. 'Was she sincere?'

Grace nodded. 'Yes. We all believed her. I think she's had a tough life so far and within the space of a few days, Sandy and Sonia made her feel she was part of a family, and that's when the guilt and remorse set in.'

Hope laughed. 'Those two could turn a murderer into a saint. So has everyone agreed then?'

'Yep. Griff said everyone deserves a second chance. He also said that he thinks it's best if we don't mention this to anyone else. So please don't repeat this, okay? I'm telling you this in confidence. Some of the villagers might not feel quite as lenient, so Griff's intending to tell people that he's heard the perpetrator was from London and the chances of this ever happening again are practically zero. But he told the girl in no uncertain terms that if she put a foot wrong from hereon, he would personally take her to the police station in Folkestone. He also said that if she proved that she could really be trusted, he'd buy her a bicycle of her own. I've never seen anyone as happy as she was. But this is the best bit. Guess what her name is. I haven't said it because I think it's so ironic. No. You'll never guess. It's–'

'Honesty?' Hope said.

Grace's eyes opened wide. 'How did you know that?'

'Just a hunch. Now isn't it time we actually got on with this meeting? It won't be long before lunch is ready.'

'Oh good heavens,' said Pat. 'And we won't be able to talk about the business once Mum's awake. She'll be constantly interrupting and asking questions, like she always does these days.'

'Right,' said Hope, opening her laptop. 'I've still got a million things to do for Fiona and Greg's wedding on Saturday, not to mention the rearranged family dinner on Friday evening in Folkestone. Although Naomi is helping me with that. And she's paying for everything.'

Grace tutted. 'Why Greg's mum is still insisting on having this celebratory meal is beyond me. Their engagement was announced six months ago. Move on, I say. Focus on the wedding.'

Greg and his mum had attempted to get the families together for this celebratory meal several times during the six months after he proposed, but Greg's family was large and exceedingly busy. Time, other commitments, and finding a suitable venue had proved difficult. Greg had six siblings, most of whom had partners of their own and some of whom had kids, and both his parents also came from large families, which meant aunts and uncles and cousins, galore. His mum wanted an early evening seating so that all the children could attend and still be home in time for bed, but as several came from a distance away, that too was an issue. They had eventually found a restaurant and all had gone well – until Naomi's car had broken down on her way to Betancourt Bay and the restaurant in Folkestone. Fortunately, this same restaurant had already been booked for the wedding reception, and, when there was a last-minute cancellation by another large party, for the Friday night, Eversley Events had snapped it up on behalf of Greg and his mum. Although as Naomi was now paying for it all, she was really their client for that particular event.

'Tell me about it,' said Hope. 'But between us, Fiona's pleased his mum is so obsessed about the family get together. It's meant she's let Fi concentrate on the wedding without poking her nose in too much.'

'I bet that's another reason Fiona wanted

us,' said Grace. 'To act as a barrier between her and Greg's family. Anything they suggested, like having butterflies fly out of Greg's top hat, for example, she knew she could rely on you to veto.'

Hope rolled her eyes and shook her head. 'Fi says she still has nightmares at the thought of that. It always astonishes me just how crass some people can be. Those butterflies don't know how lucky they are to have escaped that fate.'

The wedding was taking place at St Gabriel's Church in Betancourt Bay but then it was back down to Folkestone, a few minutes' drive away for the reception and the disco at the restaurant, which meant transportation for the guests, accommodations for those who weren't local, and the nightmare of ensuring that not just one three course meal menu, but two, catered for all taste preferences and more importantly, food allergies for more than sixty people. And that was Greg and Fiona's idea of a 'small wedding'.

'Moving on,' said Simon. 'No date as yet for the Grand Opening of Betancourt Bay Café once Naomi becomes the owner, I take it.'

'Give her a chance, Dad,' said Grace. 'Griff only agreed to sell it to her this week, once Derek and Doris Dunpole's lease was officially surrendered. But the way things are moving, it won't be long. I'm tentatively saying the end of March. Easter is early this year and she wants to be open for that if possible. Griff's agreed to give her early access so she's getting started on the work required this coming week. Of course now that her new boyfriend Lucas is on the scene that could either delay things or move things forward faster. She's told him everything. All about the café and the Lottery winnings. He was shocked about the money, apparently, but delighted that Naomi plans to use it to buy the café and that she'll have a special menu to provide free meals for those who can't afford to pay. I'll keep you all updated on dates.'

'And now she also has a little criminal to help,' joked Hope.

'It'll be lovely to have the café open every day again,' said Pat.

Grace nodded. 'Naomi said she's going to employ some staff to help so that she won't have to work every day, now that she's rich enough not to have to do that.'

'Lucky for some,' said Hope. 'Although Naomi deserves her good luck at last.'

'We've got four proposals slash engagements on Valentine's Day,' said Simon.

'Really?' said Grace, sarcastically. 'How

clichéd!'

'Funny,' said Hope.

'They're all on track,' Grace confirmed. 'Just the last few minor details to deal with on the actual day, like the flowers turning up, etc.'

'And the would-be fiancés,' said Hope, winking at Grace. 'I'm meeting with Bruce Boot tomorrow to finalise the surprise eightieth birthday bash for Rita and Vera.'

The elderly Boot twins had lived in Acorn Cottage on Oak Street their entire lives. They had an older brother, Brendan who moved into Folkestone when he married, but who sadly passed away a few years ago aged seventy-nine, his beloved wife having pre-deceased him by five years. It was his son, Bruce Boot who had decided that his spinster aunts, Rita and Vera Boot deserved a birthday party.

'I'm sure they'll be overjoyed,' said Pat. 'I can't wait to see their faces.'

'I wonder why they never married,' said Grace.

'Good sense, perhaps,' said Hope.

Grace tutted and gave her a playful shove.

'You're doing the launch for Laurence's latest cosy crime novel, The Lady in the Lake, aren't you?' Simon asked Hope.

'Sadly, yes.' Hope sighed. 'Six p.m.

sharp. Laurence will give a reading and then there'll be half an hour for questions followed by the book signings, and drinks and nibbles till around eight, or when everyone leaves.'

The launch was to be held at Bishop's Books in Folkestone, which was owned by Laurence's friend, Greg Bishop who lived in Bluebell Cottage in Betancourt Bay. It was very confusing having two Greg's to deal with and more than once in recent weeks, Hope had thought she was speaking to Greg Bishop of Bishop's Books when in fact it was Greg Carter, Fiona's fiancé on the line. Not that they sounded that alike, but when you were busy it was easy to make mistakes. Now she double-checked the name or phone number of the caller before answering her phone.

She just hoped that people didn't turn up for the book launch and go to Greg Bishop's uncle's shop next door called Bishop Estate Agents. Perhaps she'd ask Greg to get his uncle to stick a notice in the window, just in case.

'Assuming Laurence doesn't bump her off first,' Grace quipped.

'I might be the one to bump him off,' Hope retorted.

Laurence Lake had purchased Seaview Cottage in the village about eight years earlier, as soon as Greg Bishop told him it was going up for sale. Laurence had used his royalties from the sales of his phenomenally successful cosy crime books and had outbid everyone. The cottage had been rented out as a holiday home for many years and all the villagers were pleased it was going to, once again, be someone's permanent home. Until the new owner started trying to bump people off – even if it was just in the pages of his books.

Hope was his latest victim for his new, as yet untitled, cosy crime novel. He was harmless enough but a bit like Russell Betancourt, Laurence was always popping up out of nowhere. Each time she saw him he had thought of a new method for her murder, and frankly, it was getting a little tiresome.

There was one man who seemed to want to show Hope his love for her was undying, and another man who loved to find new ways for her to die.

It could only happen in Betancourt Bay.

# Two

The Eversley Events meeting concluded a mere few seconds before the timer pinged to announce the beef was done. It was removed from the oven, loosely covered with tin foil, and left on the kitchen worktop to rest. The roast potatoes were turned, pots of water put on to boil for the other veg, and the Yorkshire puddings placed in one of the ovens in the Aga while an apple and blackberry crumble was placed in another.

'Anyone for sherry?' Pat offered.

'I thought you'd never ask,' Granny Joy piped up. She had an almost super-human talent to always wake up just as alcohol was mentioned, or a meal was ready.

'I'll open the wine,' said Hope, and then glanced over to Grace. 'Are you joining us today or rushing back to Griff's arms?'

Grace pulled a face. 'Griff is having lunch with his dad, step mum, and Russell, so I'm staying here out of the way.'

Griff had been saying for a while now that he had a plan regarding Bianca. Grace was clearly hoping that was what they would all be discussing today.

It wasn't that Grace was unhappy about being under the same roof as Bianca – Betancourt was big enough to avoid each other if they tried – but Bianca was continually reminding Grace, and everyone else within earshot, that Grace had believed herself to be in love with Russell for so many years.

Hope had wanted to slap Bianca when the woman asked the question in front of Hope and the rest of the Eversley family one day.

'How can you be so sure you now love Grifforde?' Bianca asked, using Griff's full name. 'And how can he be sure you won't change your mind again and fall back in love with Russell?'

'Because what I felt for Russell was a lingering, childish infatuation, and as I hardly ever saw him, it couldn't possibly be love. What I feel for Griff is completely and utterly different. And it's forever. I'm certain of that.'

Griff wrapped Grace in his arms and told Bianca that as he wasn't at all concerned about Grace's true feelings, there was really no reason for Bianca to worry. Bianca had

25

flounced off. But Grace had confided to Hope and their mum that this was a regular occurrence, although usually when Griff wasn't around to provide such love and support.

'Perhaps they'll pack Bianca off to that place she went to before Christmas,' Hope said now.

'No. That retreat was for her drink problem. As far as we know, she's remained sober since then. I think – and I hope – Griff has something more long term in mind. As soon as Naomi received her Lottery winnings, she kindly offered to pay for Bianca to take an exceedingly long holiday on a remote island in the Pacific, but I couldn't accept such an offer. Although I did mention it to Griff that night and he said it wasn't such a bad idea, but that his family would pay, not Naomi. I thought he was joking, but maybe not, so fingers crossed.'

Hope grinned as she handed her sister a large glass of red wine. 'You might want to uncross those fingers for your wine.'

Grace laughed and took the glass. 'I'll cross my toes instead.'

'When I was your age,' said Granny Joy, 'I could cross my legs behind my head. I wonder if I still can.'

'Please don't try!' Pat pleaded, as Granny Joy shifted in her chair.

'Don't try what?' Granny Joy asked, already forgetting what she'd said.

'Here's your sherry.' Simon handed her a glass.

Granny Joy peered at it and then at him. 'Are we on rations?'

She held the glass towards him and he filled it to the brim with an audible sigh.

'What's for lunch?' she asked after taking two large sips.

'Roast beef and all the trimmings,' said Grace.

'I don't want the trimmings! That's tripe you know. And that's the cow's stomach.'

'Grace didn't mean that sort of trimmings,' said Pat. 'She meant all the veg.'

'Well why didn't she say veg? Is there any sherry left in that bottle?' She emptied her glass in one gulp.

'Maybe we should send Granny Joy to that place Bianca went,' said Hope.

'Want rid of me, eh?' Granny Joy glared at Hope.

'Never, Granny. It was a joke.'

'Hmm. When's lunch ready? I'm starving. Is that dog dead?' She pointed at Lady E with one hand while knocking back the glass of sherry in her other.

Lady E was lolling in her comfy basket, but as she was emitting her usual snuffly-sounding snores, she was obviously perfectly fine.

'Perhaps I should see if she'll wake up,' said Hope, 'and take her for a quick walk before lunch.

Granny Joy tapped the basket with her foot and Lady E's eyes shot open and her bat-like ears popped up, although she looked half asleep as her dark eyes drifted from person to person.

'Time for walkies,' said Granny Joy, and Lady E leapt out of the basket, her claws skittering on the tiled floor as she raced towards the door.

'I think that's a yes then darling,' Simon said, smiling sympathetically at Hope.

'Don't be long, darling,' said Pat. 'Everything will be ready to serve in twenty minutes.'

'Don't let Granny Joy touch my wine,' said Hope taking a quick sip before placing her glass on the kitchen table and following Lady E along the wooden floor of the hall to the front door.

The lead was hanging on the hook beside the door as always and Hope grabbed her coat and scarf from the coat rack. Shrugging them on she then took her gloves from the large, black, ceramic top hat on the hall table where all the gloves were kept, and her keys from the white, ceramic bowl shaped like a bow tie.

She attached the lead to Lady E's collar and opened the front door. After the warmth in the kitchen the air outside hit her like a snowball in the face. Although it was relatively warm and sunny for a February day, compared to inside, it was freezing.

Hope shot a glance towards Betancourt but then remembered that Russell was having lunch with the family so the chances of him appearing were thankfully, remote.

She considered heading to Lookout Point and breathing in the air whilst taking in the stunning view. It was one she knew well, of course, but each day it was a little different from the day before. The sea might be a slightly lighter or darker shade of blue, green, or grey, depending on the weather, and similarly, the sky. When there were clouds, she loved studying the different shapes they made and she often saw dragons, birds, various animals, and such, drifting across the wide expanse of sky. Storm clouds were her favourite to watch though as they could look so dramatic. But even on a cloudless day, the sky was beautiful.

Lookout Point was three hundred and ten feet at its highest spot and was made up of white chalk cliffs that towered above the sand and shingle beach of Betancourt Bay. You could see Locke Isle from the top of Lookout Point – and from several other places in Betancourt Bay but if you sat on the bench at the Point on a very clear day, you could even see the coast of France.

The Lookout Steps led down to the beach but there were three hundred of them, so most people accessed the beach farther along, where the cliff paths weren't so steep and there were fewer steps.

Lady E loved running across the sand, but they didn't have time to go down to the beach right now. And besides, to get to the beach meant walking directly in sight of Seaview Cottage, and Laurence might be sitting in his study at the front of his house, working on his new book. Hope wasn't in the mood for being murdered, and certainly not on an empty stomach.

It would also mean walking past Rosehip Cottage, home of Jean and Victor Mills, the parents of Hope's ex-boyfriend, Rob, but that didn't bother her much at all. Yes, Rob had broken her heart many years ago and it was several months before she could go anywhere near that cottage in the early days, but she could count on the fingers of one hand, the number of times since their break up that Rob had come back to visit his parents, so she had forced herself to get used to it, knowing that there was little risk of bumping into her ex.

Even on the rare occasions when he had

come home, Hope had never seen him, and he had never told her when he was around. His visits had been so fleeting in fact that his own siblings joked that if they blinked, they missed him.

All Hope knew about him was that he was still working his way around the world, no doubt having the time of his life.

Why she had suddenly thought of Rob she had no idea.

Perhaps because Grace had mentioned him the other day.

Or was it by any chance, because she had realised today that, now that Naomi had met the love of her life, Hope was the only one of the four of them who was unattached?

Grace had Griff. Fiona had Greg. And now Naomi had her handsome stranger, Lucas Dove.

Hope had no one. Unless she counted Russell Betancourt, the handsome man she didn't love but who loved her. Or Laurence Lake, the successful and equally good-looking author trying to bump her off for his new book.

And memories of Rob Mills, the one who walked away.

Oddly enough, now that she thought about it, all three men were blond.

Perhaps she attracted a certain type.

Yet the attraction wasn't reciprocated.

With the exception of Rob. Although if she saw him now she might not be attracted to him either.

She could only hope. It was inevitable that one day she would bump into him again. It was the Law of Averages.

Not that there had been anything average about Rob Mills.

'Stop thinking about Rob!' she yelled at herself, making Lady E jump and turn and give her a particularly odd look. 'Sorry sweetheart. I was yelling at myself, not you.'

She glanced around and was surprised to see the trees of East Wood stretching out before her. She had walked without paying any attention at all to the direction she was going. At least it was the opposite direction from Laurence Lake.

She let out a small sigh. The evergreens looked beautiful in the wintry sunshine and even the bare branches of the deciduous trees were stunning as they appeared to form majestic sculpture-like shapes before her eyes.

Rob liked sculpture.

'Arghh!' she hissed through clenched teeth.

She hardly ever thought of Rob these days yet suddenly she couldn't get him out of her head.

What she should be thinking about was

a magical setting for a surprise marriage proposal. And she needed to get a move on because she only had two weeks.

'I think it's time we went home, Lady E. I need wine. Lots and lots of it. And possibly a lobotomy.'

# Three

'Eversley Events. Hope speaking. How may I help you?'

Hope adopted her business voice and smiled while she spoke. Smiling while speaking on the phone was the first thing Hope learnt when she joined the family business. As unbelievable as it might seem, it genuinely did make the speaker's voice sound friendly and cheerful whether they felt that way or not.

Right now, Hope felt neither. The sun had suddenly disappeared behind a fast-moving mass of black clouds, the colour of a Raven, and now the mass hovered like some gigantic, alien spaceship above East Wood and quickly encompassed the entire village. She needed to get both herself and Lady E home before it rained cats and dogs. She loved watching rainclouds, but getting drenched – not so much. She hoped the phone call would be brief.

The family took it in turns to answer the business line on Sunday. The one they used to promote their company and for new enquiries. Once they took a client on, they gave that client their personal numbers, but they could still be contacted via the main line too. This Sunday was Hope's turn. She couldn't let it go to voicemail. Eversley Events was available eighteen hours a day, seven days a week, come rain or shine; the other six hours were for emergencies only. Hope had discovered that there seemed to be a great many 'emergencies' involved in the events planning business. Who knew? If she had, she might've chosen a different career. Getting a phone call at four a.m. from a client who couldn't sleep because they were worrying about some little detail, or had suddenly had an idea about something, was no fun.

But who in their right mind would call an event planner on Sunday at one p.m. when every sane person in the UK was either eating Sunday lunch, preparing Sunday lunch, or enjoying pre-lunch drinks?

'Oh! I expected a machine.' The male speaker on the other end of this call definitely wasn't smiling.

'Eversley Events personnel are available eighteen hours each day, seven days a week, fifty-two weeks a year.'

35

The caller snorted a laugh. 'Now that did sound like a machine. Isn't that slave labour though? And why eighteen hours?'

For a moment, Hope was taken aback. 'We have several personnel, not just one person, so no slave labour involved, I assure you. But even we need to sleep, and eighteen hours seems more than reasonable to ensure we meet, or go above and beyond, what our clients need. And I'm no machine, believe me. May I ask who's calling?'

'And yet, perhaps if you worked nineteen hours you'd be able to fit in more clients. Or even eighteen and a half.'

'That presumes we might want – or need, more clients. Which at the present time, we do not. Our diaries are full.' That sounded a little rude, but then so did this man. He definitely wasn't a client.

'Seriously? Then why not hire more staff? Surely the main purpose of an events company is to handle as many events as possible?'

'Quantity does not equate to quality.' Hope's smile was slipping and her tone was changing. She wanted to get home and she wasn't in the mood for this – whatever *this* was. 'We prefer to ensure the events we organise are managed to perfection. We've been established for fifteen years and not once have we received a complaint or a bad review.'

'Then this may not be a good day for you. I'm about to burst that bubble. You recently refused to take on a new client, despite an earlier assurance that you'd be happy to do so.'

'I ... I don't think that can be correct. We never agree to take on new clients until we have discussed it fully at one of our regular meetings. We have been so busy since Christmas that I know for a fact we have not agreed to do so.'

That wasn't entirely true. Naomi was, strictly speaking, a new client, and Eversley Events had taken on the Grand Opening of Betancourt Bay Café. And Greg and Fiona's family meal was a new event which the Eversleys hadn't been involved in planning until recently. But Fi was already a client so that didn't really count as new. And Naomi, Fi and their family were friends of the Eversleys so they were an exception to the rule.

'It was at Christmas that you agreed. At some annual bash on Christmas Eve known as the Mistletoe Dance at some stately home called Betancourt in a village by the name of Betancourt Bay. Someone named Hope Eversley said she could personally guarantee it. She told my sister to give her a call and mention the dance and they would fit her in, no problem. Wait. Didn't you say your name was Hope when you answered my call? Are you Hope Eversley?'

Hope swallowed to clear a lump forming in her throat, and was about to say she did no such thing when a faint and distant memory pervaded her thoughts.

Damn it. Why had she had so much to drink at the Mistletoe Dance? Okay, she was dealing with the bombshell of Russell declaring his love for her, and also toasting the news that Grace and Griff were now an item, not to mention the fact that the entire family was celebrating the success of the night itself for their business. Plus, Christmas was the season to be jolly, after all. Besides all that, she was, technically, off the clock that night. But even so.

'I ... I.' She had to face the music. She raised her head and stuck out her chin – not that the caller could see that. 'Yes. This is Hope Eversley.' Then the heavens opened and rain bucketed down on her and Lady E. 'Arghh!' She hadn't meant to let out that startled shriek.

'Are you all right? I'm cross, but I didn't intend to upset you that much.' He sounded sincere and there was genuine concern in his rather delectable voice.

'You haven't,' said Hope. 'I'm outside and it's pouring hard.' That wasn't terribly professional. She forced the smile back in place despite ice cold raindrops streaming down her cheeks. 'Erm. I'm afraid I must end this call as something has come up. If you text me your name, and the number I can reach you on, in say ... ten minutes, I will call you back so that we can clear up this misunderstanding. Thank you for calling Eversley Events.' Without waiting for his reply, Hope rang off, scooped Lady E up into her arms and ran for home.

'Hope! Hope, wait!'

Hope recognised the voice above the drumming rain as she raced past The Royal Oak, but she wasn't going to stop and chat in this weather. Although being bumped off by Laurence, who had obviously been leaving the pub as she rushed by, might not be such a bad idea right now. It was probably a better prospect than appeasing a disgruntled, formerly potential new client.

'Can't stop now,' she yelled without looking back and heaved a sigh of relief as she shoved open the pink front door of The White House a few moments later.

'Now who's late?' Grace yelled from the kitchen and popped her head out into the hall. 'Where have you been? We've been trying to call you for the last five minutes. We're waiting to dish up lunch.'

Hope put Lady E down, removed the

lead and hung it on the hook. Then she tossed her keys in the bow tie bowl, placed her phone on the hall table, pulled off her sodden coat and scarf, and glared at Grace as Lady E shook herself and skittered along the hall.

'I lost track of time. I'm soaked, as you can no doubt see. And I need to make a call. Put mine on a plate and leave it in the oven, please. I'll be there as soon as I can. Oh, and can you dry off the dog?'

'You okay?' Grace asked, sounding concerned as Lady E dashed to her water bowl in the kitchen.

'Yeah. Just a little misunderstanding I need to sort out. Give me ten minutes.'

Hope kicked off her wet shoes, peeled off the saturated socks, and ran upstairs to her room, stopping halfway to come back down and retrieve her phone from the hall table.

'Anything I can help with?' Grace asked, still lingering in the hall.

'Not unless you have a magic wand and can turn back time.'

'That's a no then. I'll tell Mum you won't be long.'

Hope ran into her en suite bathroom, tossed her wet socks into the linen basket in the corner, and stripped off her damp clothes. She would have loved a hot shower but she didn't have time. Her phone had beeped with a text as she was running home and she needed to be true to her word and make that call.

She dried herself with the towel that was hanging on the heated rail and quickly threw on a pair of track suit bottoms and a baggy, wool jumper. Thank God this wasn't going to be a video call. She looked positively bedraggled. She pulled her wet hair into a loose bun, sat on her bed, took several deep breaths and then with a smile plastered on her face, read the text.

He could not be serious. Hope almost burst out laughing when she saw the name of her mystery caller.

But, Holy Hell. What if it *was* him?

Did Tom Hardy even have a sister?

Of course it wasn't *that* Tom Hardy. There must be lots of Toms with the same name.

Wait. That didn't sound quite right. Thank goodness she hadn't said that to him!

Only one way to find out. She called the number he'd given and recognised the voice immediately.

'Is that Hope?' She had called him from her own number, not the business line.

'It is.'

'Wow. I wasn't sure you'd call back. I thought you might've just said that to get rid of me. And before you ask, no, I'm not *that*

41

Tom Hardy, the famous actor. And I'm not that good-looking, either. Plus I'm fair haired, not dark. I'm Tom Hardy, the not so famous owner of Hardy Tools.'

'Oh!' said Hope, surprised, not just by what he'd said but also because she had heard of Hardy Tools. Her dad, for one, was a fan. He said the tools were virtually indestructible, even for a DIY disaster like himself. She wasn't going to tell Tom Hardy that though.

'Mum named me after her favourite author and poet, Thomas Hardy,' he continued. 'And no. I don't resemble him either. And I can't stand his novels. I prefer a happy ending. That guy – not so much.' He gave a quick cough, as if he'd realised he was saying far too much. 'Speaking of happy endings, I hope you're going to tell me that you recall the lengthy conversation you had with my sister, Della Hardy on Christmas Eve, and that, of course you're going to take her on as a new client.'

Hope's smile was genuine as she listened to the deep almost sultry voice – until that last sentence. She had never been a fan of Thomas Hardy's work and as ridiculous as it was, it pleased her that this man wasn't either. She also liked the way he had explained how he'd been given his name. He sounded as if he had a sense of humour.

Sadly, his final sentence brought her back to reality.

'Erm.' She cleared her throat. 'I do recall having a conversation with your sister, but I must explain that it was Christmas Eve, I wasn't in work mode, and I'm fairly certain I didn't actually promise that we would take her on as a client. I would never do that no matter how drunk ... I mean ... no matter what the situation. Having said that, I apologise if there was a misunderstanding. I want to do everything I can to help. Eversley Events is not in the business of letting people down, however innocently that possibility may have arisen. We're here to help people achieve their dream event. So perhaps, if you could give me some details of the event your sister wanted us to organise, I may have some ideas as to how we can resolve this matter.'

He didn't reply right away, and when he did, he sort of sniggered. 'You were drunk?'

'No! Well. Possibly tipsy. It was Christmas Eve, remember.'

'I know. Della didn't tell me that you might've been six sheets to the wind.'

'I wasn't!' Damn. She should've said she was. Being drunk might've been an excuse – although not a good one. 'I never get that drunk.'

'Then you're confirming you were sober

enough to discuss business? Della is adamant that you had a lengthy conversation and that you said you'd be happy to take her on and could fulfil her dream, no problem. So much so that she hasn't bothered to look at any other company. She said she liked you right away and she knew you would be the perfect person to make her dream come true. I know you said you're busy, but surely you could squeeze one more event into your hectic schedule and let my sister have her dream, couldn't you? It would mean a lot to me if you did. And yes, that is my way of saying you can name your price. Within reason. I'm in business too and I know when I'm being ripped off. But Della's happiness is important to me. So will you do it?'

Hope was so enthralled by the timbre of his voice and captivated by the sincerity and love in his words that she needed a moment to regain her composure. That did sound like something she might say after a few drinks, and she made a mental note never to drink and discuss business at the same time, again.

'You still haven't told me what the event is. I can't agree to anything until I know that.'

'Unless you're drunk. Sorry. Tipsy.' He laughed.

'And just as we were starting to get along so well.' Hope matched his now teasing tone as she leant back against the pillows on her bed.

His laugh made her skin tingle with excitement and she wondered what he looked like. He'd said he was fair, not dark, so blond, perhaps?

Oh God. Not another blond-haired man in her life. She had quite enough of those already.

He sounded a similar age to Russell and Laurence, so in his thirties she presumed. But could you really tell a person's age from their tone of voice?

'You're easy to talk to,' he said. 'I thought I might have a fight on my hands, but it sounds as if you really do want to try to help. Thank you, Hope.'

Was he wondering about her?

She pulled herself to an upright sitting position. This was work. She shouldn't be flirting and she certainly shouldn't be imagining if he was as handsome as he sounded.

'I do. But the fact that you appear to be reluctant to tell me what this event is, makes me think it is not as simple as one that we could 'just squeeze in'. Or am I wrong?'

He gave a small cough. 'The thing is, Della is a bit of a dreamer. And although, as I said, she is adamant you agreed and that she told you all about it at the dance on Christmas Eve, I am willing to admit that she should've contacted you long before last week. Especially as she should've taken into account that you might have had a few drinks when you said that it wouldn't be a problem.'

'You're not instilling confidence as to its simplicity. Just tell me what it is. I can't help if I don't know.'

'Okay. It's a leap year this year and–'

'No!' Hope interrupted. 'Please don't tell me that she wants to propose to her boyfriend. And definitely don't tell me she wants to do so on Valentine's Day.'

'No,' he said, and Hope sighed with relief. But it was short-lived. 'She wants to propose to her girlfriend. And yes. On Valentine's Day. Although as they're both female I can't see how this leap year thing is relevant. But once Della gets an idea in her head there's no stopping her. She wants the room to look like a fairy grotto. Oh, and she wants to arrive on a white horse. Because–'

'Because,' Hope stopped him again, 'unfortunately, unicorns don't exist.'

Hope closed her eyes and fell back against the pillows again.

'Did you just read my mind? Or do you now recall the conversation with Della?'

Hope let out the longest sigh. 'Should I call you on this number? Or do you want to give me Della's so that I can speak with her direct? I assume you're not local from what you said in our first conversation. Is Della?'

'That depends where "local" is. Your website doesn't say where you're based, merely that it's in South East England, and Della didn't tell me. I live in Bournemouth, so no. Della moved in with her girlfriend at the New Year and they live in Folkestone.'

'Folkestone is local.'

'Great. But since there's been a bit of a mix up so far, I think I should take control initially, so please call me. Are you saying you'll do it? Valentine's Day is only ten days away.' He sounded anxious now.

'I'm well aware of that, Tom. Leave it with me. I'll see what I can do and I'll give you a call on Monday.'

'Thank you, Hope. You're aptly named.'

# Four

'The cat's out of the bag, I'm afraid.' Bruce Boot sounded both relieved and disappointed in equal measure when he phoned Hope at eight-thirty on Monday morning. 'But I suppose at least this way my aunts can have a say in how they want their birthday party to go.'

Hope was tempted to say, 'No they can't! Not at this late stage.' Instead she said, 'Of course.'

'It also means we can have our meeting in Acorn Cottage instead of at my house. That'll save you some time. I'm here already.'

Hope swallowed the curse that was about to come out of her mouth, and turned her car around to head back to Betancourt Bay. She'd left early to ensure she arrived on time as Bruce lived on the other side of Folkestone. Monday morning traffic in Folkestone could mean lengthy delays, but the traffic was light this morning and she had planned to park nearby and sit and enjoy the steaming cup of coffee she had just bought. She could forget that now.

'Absolutely. I'll see you at nine as planned. Although please don't worry if I'm a minute or two late. We've had some urgent things to deal with this morning.'

'Not a problem,' said Bruce. 'I was going to call you yesterday, but I didn't want to bother you on a Sunday. We all need some time off. I stayed here last night, and that's how they found out. Silly old me. I left the list I wanted to go through with you open on my laptop while I went to the loo.' He giggled like a naughty child.

Hope was less amused. 'Oh dear. Well never mind. I'll see you soon.'

'No rush if you've got things to do. It'll give my aunts more time to decide on what they want.'

Hope pushed her foot down hard on the accelerator. The less time they had to do that, the better it would be for her. The way things were going she wouldn't be at all surprised if Rita and Vera Boot decided they also wanted a unicorn. Or maybe a choir of elves to sing Happy Birthday to them.

Although that wasn't necessarily impossible. Obviously, elves – like unicorns – didn't exist. But children's choirs did. And it was easy enough to get elven costumes.

Especially in February. Unless they wanted to go for the whole Lord of the Rings type of thing. But even those were fairly easy to acquire. Perhaps she would suggest it to them. Before they got too many ideas of their own.

'Bye for now,' she said, ringing off and instantly calling home. 'Change of plan. I'm now meeting Bruce at Acorn Cottage.'

'Who's this?' It was Granny Joy's voice.

That was all Hope needed this morning.

'Hi Granny. It's Hope. Is Mum there?'

'Yes,' she said, and promptly hung up.

Hope almost laughed but it wasn't really funny. The quicker that damn tumour in Granny Joy's head shrunk, the happier everyone would be. And not just because, despite all the reassurances from the consultants that Granny Joy would be fine and the tumour was benign, until they were given the news that the thing had gone or at least was small enough not to be a problem, none of them would stop worrying.

The consultant Griff had arranged for her was fantastic and the treatment was going well. Hopefully it wouldn't be too long before they could see and hear the results. Granny Joy wasn't herself right now and the sooner she got back to normal the better it would obviously be. She would get her life back. She might even be able to return to her own home in Folkestone and her lovely neighbours. Although they all visited her at The White House fairly regularly.

But perhaps it would be best if Granny Joy stayed at The White House permanently. Or maybe not. They'd all have to wait and see. For now, Hope would try to call her mum again. This time she got through.

'Why did you let Granny answer your phone?'

'I didn't.'

'Well she did. I called you less than five minutes ago and she answered and then hung up on me when I asked if you were there.'

Pat tutted. 'I'll remember to take it with me to the loo next time.'

Now Hope did laugh. 'Why is everyone telling me about their trips to the loo this morning?'

'What, darling?'

'Never mind. I'm calling to tell you there's been a change of plan and I'm meeting Bruce at Acorn Cottage.'

'So you'll be home sooner than you thought?'

'I wouldn't bank on that. Rita and Vera have found out about the party and they may have some input, it seems. I could be longer than I'd planned. Have you heard from Grace?'

'Not yet. But she's got that meeting with the Hamiltons this morning, about their daughter's wedding, so I expect she's on her way to that.'

'I know. But I thought she'd call and let us know whether anything's happened regarding Bianca. Maybe the Betancourts weren't discussing that yesterday after all.'

'Maybe not. I'm sure she'll tell us if there's any news. Will you be home for lunch?'

Hope laughed. 'I certainly hope so. If the Boots keep me there beyond twelve, I may lose the will to live. Any luck with that unicorn?'

'Not yet. But your dad and I are still looking.'

'Okay. Let me know if you have any success. See you later.'

Hope's family hadn't been best pleased when Hope had told them yesterday at lunch that she'd just taken on a new client, and even less so when she gave them the details.

'A unicorn?' said Grace. 'She does know they're not real, right?'

'Of course she does.'

'And a fairy grotto?' Pat shook her head. 'There's a lot of work involved in that.'

'Tom said cost isn't an issue. Within reason.'

'You've gone red,' said Grace. 'What

aren't you telling us?'

'What?' Hope's startled gaze darted around the table and all eyes were now on her. 'Nothing. Honestly. I ... I'm just a bit embarrassed about how this happened, that's all.'

'Oh, don't give that another thought, darling,' said Pat. 'We've all had a little too much to drink from time to time and said things we perhaps shouldn't have. It was Christmas Eve, so it really wasn't your fault. The girl should've contacted us before last week in any case. But we'll manage, so don't worry. Finding a unicorn and a fairy grotto may be time consuming but it can't be that difficult.'

'There's a fairy grotto in next door's garden,' said Granny Joy, pointing her knife in the direction of The Rectory, and all eyes turned to her. 'I saw them all dancing out there last night.'

Hope grinned. 'Problem solved then. I'll pop next door and ask the vicar if we can hire them.'

'Do you mean Reverend Copeland and his wife Daisy?' queried Simon.

'I think she means the garden gnomes,' said Pat.

'They were Fairies,' Granny Joy snapped. 'I saw them with my own eyes.' She glanced towards the Eversley's own garden.

'Just as clearly as I can see that unicorn out there, sheltering under the apple tree.'

The rest of the family exchanged sympathetic glances.

'Oh yes,' said Hope. 'Now eat your lunch before it gets cold, Granny.'

Hope couldn't give Della Hardy a real-life unicorn as there weren't any – despite what Granny Joy had said yesterday – but she could give her the next best thing. A white horse with a white cone shaped cardboard cut-out on its forehead for the horn, secured in position with white ribbons and a white bridle.

Unfortunately, there seemed to be a shortage of white horses nearby and the family were now having to search further afield. Hope had spent most of yesterday afternoon on the internet with no luck.

Then there was the small matter of the fairy grotto to consider. And there definitely wasn't one of those in the Reverend Brian Copeland's back garden.

Hope growled under her breath. Why couldn't people simply be happy with a posh restaurant, a bottle of champagne, and the ring inside a specially made dessert, or something?

But then Eversley Events wouldn't be raking in all the money that they were right now. Although money wasn't everything.

Sanity was more valuable.

Which reminded her that she still needed to find a magical setting for that other surprise proposal. And if this morning was anything to go by, a living, breathing, real life unicorn might be easier to come by.

Thankfully the traffic was still light and Hope drove past her home on Folkestone Road and turned into Oak Street, pulling up outside Acorn Cottage at five minutes to nine. She took a deep breath and was about to step out of her car when her mobile rang and she saw it was Grace. She closed the door and answered.

'I know you're meeting Bruce Boot,' said Grace, 'but have you got five minutes?'

'For you? Always. Are you okay? I thought we might hear from you last night. Or early this morning.'

'I know. It was a crazy evening and I didn't get a chance to call earlier. I've been trying you for ages but you've been constantly engaged, and before that, I couldn't get a signal. Did you know the Hamiltons live in the middle of nowhere?'

'Yes. Didn't you?'

'I do now. And I also understand why the bride-to-be said she'd be leaving this house by tractor. And will not be coming back.'

Hope laughed. 'I assume you're going to try to persuade her and her parents that it might be wise to book into a hotel for the day and for her to get dressed in luxurious surroundings and then have a limousine – or if they insist, that appropriately decorated tractor, transport her to the church from there.'

'Yep. I know they had their hearts set on her leaving from their front door, because it's an ancient, family tradition, but having finally seen the said front door, I think it's a no-no. I can't even begin to imagine what it'll look like in the wedding photos. Not even the best photo editing software on the planet could make this front door look ... decent. I'll send you a photo so that you can see it in all its ... whatever it is. Because it certainly isn't glory.'

'I'll look forward to that. But what happened yesterday? That's what I really want to know.'

'All hell broke loose.'

'What? Oh no. Are you okay? How's Griff?'

'We're both fine. Archie, however, is not. Bianca decided that actions speak louder than words. And she had a lot to ... say. I think the plate of food over his head in the restaurant said that she thinks he's a jerk and she wanted everyone to know it. And throwing all his clothes out of his bedroom window when they got home, said she was upset, I believe. But giving him a black eye by hitting him with her handbag, just says she's a nasty piece of work, in my opinion.'

'Blimey, Grace! Did she really do all that?'

'And more, apparently. I saw the clothes and the handbag parts myself.'

'What did Griff and Russell do?'

'In the restaurant, not much, apart from try to calm her down. Once they were back home, they both did their best. But although they knew she was ... volatile, I don't think either of them thought she would go that far, and it was too late to stop her by the time they realised Archie's clothes were flying through the air. The whack with her handbag, none of us saw coming. They did manage to stop her from doing any further harm though, and by about eleven last night, she was calm enough for them to send her away in a chauffeur driven car. But I'm not sure any of us got much sleep last night. Every time I heard a noise, I kept thinking it was her, coming back to say a bit more, and I woke Griff up several times to check.'

'Wow. Is that it then? Has she gone for good? And where did they send her?'

'Archie's going to start divorce proceedings as soon as possible. Griff says there's no way he'll have her in the house again, and all the staff knows that. As for where she went, to a friend's house, according to Griff.'

'I didn't know she had any friends.'

'No. Nor did I. Anyway, she's gone and that's what matters. And this is the best bit. The first thing Griff said to me when we woke up this morning ... wait. No. Not the first thing.' Grace laughed. 'I can't tell you the first thing he said.'

'I get the picture, thanks. Moving on.'

'Okay. The second thing he said was that now Bianca isn't around, will I reconsider moving in with him. So you see. He isn't having doubts.'

'I didn't say he was. And I'm really happy for you. I assume you said yes.'

'Too bloody right I did! I'm telling Mum and Dad when I've finished here, but I wasn't sure when I'd see you today and I wanted you to be the first to know.'

'I'll see you at home at lunchtime, if you're there. My meeting with the Boots is now in Betancourt Bay, so I'm already here, and I won't be spending an hour or two shopping in Folkestone. And I'd better go, or I'll be late. Congratulations, Grace. I'm so pleased everything is working out for you.'

'Thanks. Me too. Now if you would fall in love with Russell, we could both live here.'

'Goodbye Grace.' Hope hung up, shook her head, stepped out of her car, and marched the few steps to Acorn Cottage.

Bruce Boot beamed at her when he opened the front door.

'Right on time,' he said. 'I've just put the kettle on. Come in.'

Hope followed him inside and it was like stepping back in time. She'd been inside this cottage a few times before, but not for years, and she'd forgotten that it looked as if it hadn't been decorated since the second World War.

'Well isn't this exciting?' Rita Boot said as soon as Bruce showed Hope into their quaint but equally antiquated sitting room.

'We had no idea,' said Vera. 'Until the dear boy left his laptop open.'

'And we had to peek,' said Rita.

'Who wouldn't?' queried Vera.

'We shouldn't have really,' Rita frowned.

'You're quite right dear,' said Vera. 'He might've been watching a porno.'

Hope nearly choked.

'Are you all right, dear?' Rita asked.

'Get her a glass of water,' ordered Vera.

Bruce went off and did so without batting an eyelid at their comment about the porno.

'Do sit down.'

Rita pointed to an armchair near the fire and then she and Vera sat on the sofa opposite leaving just enough space for Bruce to squash in beside them.

'Thank you,' said Hope as he handed her the water.

She took a few small sips and then placed the glass on a coaster on the antique side table next to her chair.

'Budge up,' said Bruce, grinning at his aunts as he settled down beside Vera.

'Now that it's not a surprise,' Hope began, 'is there anything you'd like to ask me about your eightieth birthday party?' She smiled when Rita and Vera both raised their hands. 'You don't need to raise your hands, ladies. Just say whatever is on your mind.'

The sisters exchanged glances and in unison asked, 'Can we have some dancers?'

'Dancers? Yes of course. What sort of dancers? Ballroom? Ballet?'

'Male dancers!' The elderly ladies both said. 'The ones who take off their clothes.'

# Five

'You're joking!'

Grace couldn't stop laughing when Hope joined her family at lunch and told them about the tweaks the Boot sisters had made to what was previously a rather small and sedate event.

'I'm not. Male strippers weren't the only request. They want a mini casino, or at the very least, a roulette wheel and a poker table.'

'Strip poker, no doubt,' Pat said, shaking with amusement as she placed a pot filled with steaming hot tomato soup on the large iron trivet at the centre of the kitchen table.

'It's always the quiet ones,' said Simon, removing freshly baked bread from the Aga and setting it on a bread board to cool a little.

'They've invited Granny Joy,' Hope added, taking the breadboard from her dad's hands and making room for it beside the pot of soup.

'Why doesn't that surprise me?' Pat said.

She sat down and served the soup to each member of the family, starting with her own mum.

'What's this?' asked Granny Joy.

'It's tomato soup, Mum.'

'Looks like a bowl ketchup. Don't hog that bread, Hope. Cut me a slice. Door-stop sized.'

Hope did as she was told. 'I'm just waiting for the call to tell me they've decided they also want a bucking broncho and a mud wrestling ring.'

'Don't joke about such things,' said Simon.

When Hope's phone rang right at that moment, they all looked at one another and burst out laughing.

But it wasn't the Boot sisters. It was Della Hardy.

'Hello, Hope,' she said. 'It's Della. Della Hardy.'

'Hello Della. How are you?' Hope shot an apologetic look at Pat.

'Erm. Fine thanks. I … I'm just calling to say I'm sorry. I hope you don't mind. You wrote your direct line number on the card you gave me on Christmas Eve. Tom told me he spoke to you yesterday.'

'He did. But there's no need to apologise. It was simply a misunderstanding.'

'I know. But I wanted you to know that I

didn't ask him to call you and I didn't give him your phone number. He did that off his own bat. I was telling him how disappointed I was because I wouldn't be able to do the proposal the way I wanted and I got upset. He asked why not and I told him that when I called you last week, a woman told me you were too busy to take on new clients. I should've known he'd find your website and call. He's always been protective of me. He's thirteen years older, and when our parents died, he brought me up. He thinks he needs to be my dad as well as my brother. If I wanted the moon he'd try to get it for me. Sorry. I'm going on, aren't I? But … he told me there's a possibility that you might be able to do it after all. Is that right?'

Della's words had moved her. Now Hope knew more about Tom Hardy than she had yesterday. But something else that Della had said was niggling her.

'Erm. Yes. That is, we'll organise a surprise proposal, but whether we can get everything you're hoping for is another matter. I was going to call Tom later today with an update.'

'That's fantastic! Thank you so, so much. You don't know what this means to me.'

'I think I do. But may I ask, did you speak to me last week, Della? Only I can't recall that conversation. The one from last week, that is.

Not the one on Christmas Eve.'

'No. I'm not sure who it was but it was someone older. She said you were too busy to come to the phone and when I said that we'd met at the Mistletoe Dance and you'd said I could call you, she told me you weren't taking on new clients, and then she hung up.'

Hope sucked in a breath and glared at Granny Joy who was tucking into her soup as if she hadn't eaten for days, despite devouring a hearty breakfast of porridge followed by two slices of toast and marmalade at breakfast.

'Ah. I think I know what happened. I must apologise. The person you spoke to shouldn't have answered my phone. Sorry for the confusion.'

'Oh. That's a relief. You were so lovely and friendly when we met so I was a bit surprised because the person I spoke to last week was so ... abrupt. But Tom said I should've called much sooner anyway, and it's not really your fault. And he's right. So again, I'm sorry.'

'It's fine. Shall I still call Tom? Or would you prefer I call you now that we've sorted that out?'

'Erm. Tom, please. I'm a bit of a dreamer and I tend to get carried away. He's more down to earth and reliable. He knows exactly what I want and he'll fill me in. But I'd like to see it before the actual day, please. I promise I won't ask for any changes because I know I can trust you to make it look beautiful.'

'You'll see it before then because I'll do a mock-up on line so you'll have a better idea of what we're planning. And you can make changes, Della. It's your event. Just don't leave them until the last minute, please. And if possible, don't make too many, because this is short notice.'

'I won't. I promise.'

'I'll need to discuss a possible venue once I know what's still available. Do you have any preference?'

'No. Anywhere within a short drive of Folkestone is fine.'

'Great. Leave it with me. There're a few places in Folkestone itself that might be perfect.'

'Folkestone is lovely, isn't it? I can't wait to show Tom around. He's going to be visiting for a week or two. I want him here when I pop the question. Oooh! Maybe the three of us can meet up to make it all final or whatever. A drink would be lovely too, if you have time, that is. I know you're really busy.'

'He is? Oh yes of course we can meet up. I can definitely find time for that. We'll speak soon, Della. Bye for now.'

Hope rang off and placed her phone in front of her on the table. She was annoyed about the phone call last week but she couldn't help smiling at the prospect of meeting Tom Hardy.

Pat handed her a bowl of soup. 'It sounds as if that's all sorted.'

'It is,' said Hope, trying to dismiss Tom Hardy from her thoughts. But an alluring image was forming in her mind's eye.

What would Tom look like in the flesh?

The thought of Tom's flesh sent an unexpected ripple of excitement coursing through her entire body and soup lapped at the sides of the bowl that she was still holding aloft.

Heat shot from her chest to her neck and up into her cheeks and she hastily set the bowl down on the table.

Then she cleared her throat and added, 'I now know who Della spoke to last week. So a word of warning to everyone. From now on, never leave your mobile anywhere in this house in case a certain someone decides to answer it when it rings. Take it with you, no matter what.' She tilted her head towards Granny Joy, and the rest of the family all nodded their acknowledgement.

'I never leave my phone anywhere,' Granny Joy said, stuffing her free hand down the front of her dress and lifting out her phone from the inside of her bra.

# Six

Now that Naomi's mugger was no longer a potential threat hanging over the heads of the residents of Betancourt Bay, people felt safe to walk the streets alone at night, once again.

Not that a twelve-year-old girl was ever a real threat, but of course most of the villagers didn't know that's who the mugger was, and Griff had said it was better to keep it that way.

'The fewer people who know about Honesty's actions, the better,' he had said when Honesty had come clean about it. 'We'll say that I've had it on good authority that this was a one-off, that the perpetrator was from London, and that Naomi's belongings have been recovered. Which is completely true, so none of us will have to lie. Say nothing more than that. Honesty has told us these things herself, and she has returned the items she stole.'

Prior to Honesty's confession, Pat and Simon Eversley had insisted that they would take Lady E for her final nightly walk and that Grace and Hope must never be out alone after dark. That was a bit of a problem during those last two weeks of January and the first few days of February, because it was dark so early, and Hope had protested vehemently.

'We're grown women and we can look after ourselves. We can definitely run faster than either you or Dad if anything did ever happen.'

'Yes,' Grace had agreed. 'Hope's right.'

'Really?' Pat said. 'Naomi is your age, Grace, and look what happened to her. And that's not the point. The point is that your dad and I will be sitting here worried sick until you're home safe. Is that what you want? Your parents going grey with worry just because you two think you'll be fine?'

'Grace and I will worry about you and Dad, so what's the difference?' Hope had pointed out.

'The difference is ...' Pat had hesitated and Simon had stepped in.

'The difference is that we're your parents and it's our responsibility to keep you safe. You may be thirty, Hope and you thirty-four, Grace but you're both still our babies and we love you with all our hearts. Imagine how we'd feel if anything ever happened to either of you. We'd blame ourselves for the rest of our lives. Just do this for us, please.'

Hope had planned to say that people got mugged in daylight too, so did that mean they could never leave the house alone again? But the lines of concern on her dad's face and the worry in her mum's eyes stopped her, and both she and Grace acquiesced.

So as soon as they knew that the 'panic' was over, Hope was keen to take Lady E for a walk along the beach at night.

She loved the peace and solitude, with only the sound of the waves either gently lapping at the sand or crashing onto the shore, depending on the weather and the tides.

She loved the wide open space and often twirled around on the spot with her arms extended either side and her head raised skywards as she breathed in the stars.

She wished she could breathe them in. Sometimes they felt so close she was sure she could touch them if she tried; sometimes they seemed so far away that it made her feel small and insignificant.

She loved every second of that first walk on Monday night and so did Lady E. Until Hope remembered that she hadn't phoned Tom Hardy, as she had promised.

How could she have forgotten?

Probably because the day, which had got off to a less than promising start with the Boots rearranged meeting, had turned into the day from Hell.

Her phone had not stopped ringing, she had spilt an entire cup of tea over her laptop, and a restaurant that was booked to host a birthday party for a thirty-year-old woman and twenty female friends that very evening, had called Hope at three p.m. to say a pipe had burst and their toilets were closed due to 'flooding'.

Finding another suitable venue at such a late stage was nigh on impossible, not forgetting that all the flowers, cards and presents that had been delivered directly to the venue had to be collected from the first and transported to the second, along with the decorations, balloons, a karaoke machine, a four-tier birthday cake, a Pinata filled with specially made sweets in the shape of tiny men, and a Mariachi band.

And yet somehow she had managed it.

She had gone to the new venue minutes before the birthday girl arrived, to make sure everything was perfect, and had been invited to stay for a celebratory drink. She agreed to stay for one, and then she had been dragged to the karaoke platform by five of the thirty-year-old's friends, and made to join in with an out of tune rendition of, *I Will Always*

*Love You* – the Whitney Houston version.

Despite several attempts to leave, it was another half an hour after that that she had managed to make her excuses and escape, and had returned to The White House, had something to eat, and then headed to the beach with Lady E.

It was almost ten p.m. now. Was that too late to call?

'Hello,' he said, after only two rings. 'You weren't joking about the eighteen hours a day, were you?'

'Sadly not,' she said, ridiculously pleased to hear his voice even if he did sound a little sleepy. 'I'm sorry it's so late. I hope I didn't wake you up.'

'You did.' He laughed. 'But it's fine. I fell asleep on the sofa while watching some crime series or other. Don't ask me which one because I don't know. They all seem the same to me. That makes me sound pretty boring, doesn't it? Asleep on the sofa before ten. But it's been one of those Mondays.'

'Same here. But I haven't made it to the sofa yet.'

'Oh? Bad day?'

'Very.'

'Erm. Is that why this call's so late? Is this going to be where you tell me that you can't do Della's event after all? Were you trying to think of the best way to break it to me?'

'No! We're doing the event. I confirmed that with Della today … Oh. I'm not sure I was meant to tell you that. She called me to apologise.'

'I know. She told me.'

'That's a relief. I'd hate to be a snitch. Then she must've told you that I'd agreed to do it. And I had as good as said yes to you yesterday.' Hope's voice rose an octave. 'She told me that you're coming to Folkestone.'

'I am.' His was deliciously deep. And he was definitely smiling, she could hear it in his tone. 'I'm looking forward to it. Especially as I'm told we might be meeting up with you for a drink.'

Hope's breathing quickened and her heart fluttered in her chest. How could such an innocent sentence sound so incredibly seductive?

This man was a client. She must remain professional.

'Yes. Me too. Erm. I always like to meet clients in person before the big day, but sometimes it's not possible. We organise events throughout Sussex and beyond and we're so incredibly busy. And if there's an emergency, we have to change our plans at the last minute to deal with that.'

'I understand. I realise you've had to squeeze us in, so if you can't make it, that's fine.' His tone had changed. It was cooler now.

Forget being professional; Hope didn't want to upset this man.

'I … I didn't mean it like that. I just wanted to let you know that things happen at short notice in this business. Take today for example. My first meeting was in Folkestone so I left early to give myself plenty of time. Then I got a call from the client to say they were somewhere else, so I had to turn around and go there. My phone's been ringing all day with minor emergencies and then at three I got a call saying the restaurant that's been booked for months for a party tonight had a pipe burst and all the loos were full of sh … were flooded. I had to find another venue and then transport all the party decorations, a massive cake, loads of presents, a karaoke machine, a pinata, and a Mariachi band to the new one. It took three van-loads, all of which had to be loaded and unloaded and the new venue decorated and looking sensational by seven-thirty this evening. I got home at nine, had something to eat and now I'm walking our dog. If we'd arranged to meet tonight, it would've been a problem. And that's why I'm calling you so late.'

'And I thought my day was bad,' he said after a moment's silence. 'I'm sorry, Hope.'

'It's not your fault. I'm sorry for

dumping all that on you. Why was your day bad?'

'Compared to yours, it wasn't. I'm dealing with a messy divorce that–'

'You're married!' Why hadn't it occurred to her that he might be?

'What? No. Not my divorce. I'm not married. Or dating. I'm single. Totally single. Erm. It's a divorce that's stopping the sale of a small business that I'm trying to buy. It means I'm having to negotiate with both the wife and the husband as they jointly own it. They hate one another so it's a total pain and I decided today that I may have to walk away from it.'

'I see.' She hoped he hadn't heard the sigh of relief. 'I'm sorry. That must be annoying.'

'It is. But these things happen. Erm. What about you?'

'Me?'

'Married? Dating? Single? You said earlier, 'our dog'. Are you living with someone?'

'Yes,' she teased. 'My entire family and our dog. Although my sister will be moving in with her boyfriend this week. But no significant other for me.'

'So we're both single.'

'Living miles apart.'

'Distance, like age, is just a number,

Hope. How old are you by the way? Or is it rude to ask a woman her age?'

'It's incredibly rude.' She laughed. 'But I'm thirty. You?'

'Thirty-three. I'm thirteen years older than Della.' He gave a small cough. 'I'd better let you go. Can I ... can I call you tomorrow? For an update of course.'

'An update? Oh. The proposal. Yes. I'm afraid we haven't been able to find a white horse yet but we're still looking. My sister's boyfriend may be able to help. He's got a lot of contacts. Whatever happens, I'll make sure that Della's day is magical. You can trust me on that.'

'I do. Sleep well, Hope.'

'And you, Tom. Goodnight.'

Hope rang off, held her phone to her chest, and gave a little scream of delight.

It was only then that she realised she couldn't see Lady E.

# Seven

Although it was a clear, cold night when Hope had set out, a sea fog was now rolling in obscuring the light from the moon and cloaking the incoming tide. How had she not noticed? She'd been so captivated by Tom's voice yet again that it was as if she had been in another world.

'Lady E!' she shrieked, panic rising in her voice as the beach was quickly becoming enveloped by the fog. 'Lady Elizabeth! Come!'

She ran towards the sea but there was no sign of the little dog so she turned and ran back towards the cliffs. What with the fog, and the only available light given off by the moon now hidden, Hope couldn't see more than a few feet in front of her. And just when she needed the torch on her mobile phone, it lasted all of two minutes before the battery died. She hadn't charged it at all today and it had been in constant use.

Fortunately she knew Betancourt Bay like the back of her hand and could find her way home in the pitch black if necessary. But she wasn't going anywhere without Lady E.

She called out again, even louder this time, and her heart swelled with relief when she heard a muffled yap. A moment later Lady E trotted towards her with what appeared to be a length of seaweed in her mouth.

'Where did you go?' Hope said, scooping up the little dog and hugging her, seaweed and all. 'I think we should get home, don't you?'

Hope hurried up the three hundred steps to Lookout Point and only then did she deposit Lady E on the ground, keeping a tight hold of the lead, just in case. The sea fog followed steadily behind her, creeping inch by inch over Betancourt Bay.

The grass on Lookout Point was still sodden in places from the torrential rain on Sunday so Hope made for the road; the risk of being seen by Laurence Lake as she hurried past his cottage being slightly preferable to muddy paws and little legs, not to mention her own boots.

She made it along Betancourt Street and had just turned into Folkestone Road when she heard the footsteps behind her. She knew it wasn't a mugger – unless another had come to the village, which of course was highly unlikely, and she knew it was probably someone she knew, but nevertheless it unnerved her for some reason. No doubt due to the fog and the fact that even though she was less than fifty feet from home, she couldn't see The White House.

The hand on her shoulder made her scream and she turned and lashed out instinctively.

'Oww!' her assailant moaned. 'That hurt.'

'Laurence?' Hope peered at him as he held his nose.

'Is it bleeding?' he tilted his head up.

'No. But it would serve you right. What were you thinking, creeping up on me in this fog?'

'I wasn't creeping. I was running. But I've got my slippers on.'

He glanced down at his 'Grandad' slippers and Hope sniggered as she followed his gaze, taking in his striped pyjamas, and the vintage smoking jacket over the top of them.

'Very chic,' she said.

He pulled a face. 'I was working, okay? I like to be comfortable. I was just thinking about you, and suddenly there you were, right outside my window.'

'And you felt you had to come and tell me

that?'

'No. I saw you in the fog – only I wasn't sure it was you at first and had to do a double take. I realised sea fog – or any fog – is the perfect cover. But even better. What if I killed the wrong person? Maybe you have the same coat as them, or something? What do you think?'

'I think you're slightly insane. But that happens in that old movie, *Footsteps in the Fog*. It's one of Granny Joy's favourites. The man tries to kill his maid in the fog, but he kills someone else by mistake.'

Laurence ignored her, 'I think it would be an added twist. I'm planning to kill you off with poisonous fungi. You'll be foraging in the woods for mushrooms to make a soup. Or to add to a stew. I haven't decided on the menu yet.' He waved a hand dismissively. 'My killer has been watching you, and follows you home, and waits, then adds the lethal ingredient to the pot that's sitting on the stove. Maybe through an open window. Or the killer could sneak into your kitchen when you're in another room.'

'I'll remember to close all windows and lock all doors in future,' Hope said.

'Death cap or destroying angel would do the trick. I've done some research on both. Just one bite is enough to do the job. Death cap causes most deaths, worldwide, but destroying angel has that certain ring, don't you think?'

'Oh, absolutely. It's all in the name.'

'I agree. And it would make a good title too.' He held his hand up like a sort of claw and slowly traced a banner in the air, the swirl of fog as he did so made it all seem slightly surreal. 'Destroying Angel by Laurence Lake. I can see it now.'

'Me too. But I really must get home.'

'I'll walk with you.' He dropped his hand and linked his arm through Hope's, ensuring he was on the side closest to the road, Lady E being nearest to the houses. 'Death cap causes kidney and liver failure. Severe abdominal pain, vomiting, and diarrhoea occur within six to twenty-four hours after ingestion, and that's followed by jaundice, seizures, coma, and finally, death.' His smile was far too wide for someone discussing such a grizzly demise of another human being. 'Destroying angel is similar but symptoms are usually within eight to twenty-four hours, and after the pain, sickness and diarrhoea, there's often a period of time when the person thinks they're going to be okay. And then ... WHAM!' he clapped his hands together like a pair of cymbals. 'Liver and kidney failure kick in and you're a gonna.'

'How delightful!' Hope threw him a suitably disgusted look.

'Only a few people have survived. Sadly, you won't be one of them. I do so love it when one of the main characters is bumped off. Don't worry. You'll live for most of the book. I was going to use the little devils in a previous book, but changed my mind because it was set in a city. This one's set in a village like Betancourt Bay, and there's a lot of woodland, and hills, so it's perfect for foraging.'

Hope snorted derisively as they reached the pink front door of her home, barely visible in the fog.

'It's as if you don't know me at all, Laurence. Me? Foraging? The only foraging I do is for biscuits and cakes in my parents' kitchen. That's about as wild as it gets. But hey. You do what you've gotta do. The less like me this character is, the better. Good night, Laurence.'

'Pleasant dreams, Hope.'

'Yeah right,' she said. 'I'll probably be having nightmares after all of that.'

# Eight

Hope had slept fitfully, but it wasn't due to nightmares. It was dreams of Tom Hardy that had kept her tossing and turning for several hours, and she woke up covered in sweat.

Whatever she and Tom had been doing in her dreams must have been ... extremely energetic.

Despite being alone in her bedroom, she flushed as memories of some of it raced to the forefront of her mind and she tilted her head from side to side as if replaying scenes from the night. Was that position even possible? She grinned broadly and her heart thumped in her chest at the prospect of potentially finding out.

'Hope!' Pat yelled up the stairs. 'Are you ever getting up this morning? Grace has been trying to call you. Griff has found a white horse.'

Hope sat bolt upright. 'Damn it.' She had

forgotten to put her phone on charge last night. But it was great news about the horse. She would phone Tom and ... no. She would wait. She still had the fairy grotto to sort out. And a venue to put it in. Plus she had told Tom several times how busy they were. If she called him every five minutes, he'd either think she was a liar, or that he was special.

'Did you hear me, Hope?'

Hope threw off her duvet and jumped out of bed. 'The whole of Betancourt Bay heard you, Mum. I'll be down in ten minutes.'

She showered, dressed and was in the kitchen in nine, and she plonked herself down on a vacant chair and let out a sigh.

'Remind me my phone is on charge in the hall. Please don't let me leave without it.'

Pat raised an eyebrow as she poured Hope a cup of coffee. 'Didn't you say we should have our phones with us at all times, no matter what?'

Hope met Pat's eye and without a word, leapt up and raced along the hall, retuning with her phone a moment later. She placed it on one of the many charging pads scattered throughout the house, this one being on the kitchen worktop next to the bread bin. She stood on guard beside it, leaning against the counter, a few feet away from her dad.

'Thanks, Mum,' she said, taking the cup of coffee Pat had poured for her. 'And not just for the coffee.' She grinned and took a long drink before adding, 'So where's this horse then?'

'It's under the apple tree in the garden,' said Granny Joy who was seated in her usual chair alongside Lady E, who was sleeping in her basket by the Aga.

'With the unicorn?' Hope joked.

Granny Joy tutted loudly and frowned at her. 'Don't be silly, Hope. Unicorns don't exist. You're such a dreamer.'

'It's at a stable yard fifteen miles from here owned by a friend of Griff's,' said Pat. 'Grace has forwarded a photo and it's so beautiful you could almost believe it was a unicorn.' She picked up her own phone and scrolled. 'It's an Andalusian mare and its name is Brilliant Day. Isn't that simply perfect? Look.'

Hope took the phone and was mesmerised by the photo. This horse could have stepped out from the screen of a mythical movie. Her mane was long and glossy and fell across her forehead like a veil. Her tail was full, long, and lustrous and her coat shimmered in the sunlight as she stood with her head erect and her eyes bright.

She was nothing short of magnificent. And would no doubt cost a fortune to hire. But Tom had said that cost wasn't an issue. Within reason.

'She's perfect,' said Hope with a slight catch in her voice.

She almost envied Della being able to ride Brilliant Day. Assuming they could agree a price, sort out the insurance, transport the horse to wherever the proposal was going to take place, keep her safe throughout, and then transport her back to the stable yard unscathed and untroubled.

'Now all we need is the fairy grotto, and that's another one in the bag,' said Simon, who was currently making toast.

'In the bag?' Pat laughed. 'Ever the romantic, darling.'

He grinned and blew his wife a kiss.

Pat moved closer and gave him a playful shove with her hip.

He pulled her into his arms and twirled her around.

'Get a room,' said Hope.

But she couldn't help smiling as they kissed each other briefly on the lips, and waltzed around the kitchen only stopping when the toaster pinged to announce the toast was done.

'Someone's at the door,' Granny Joy declared. 'And we all know it won't be Bert.'

Bert was their postman and as he never appeared until at least eleven a.m. Granny Joy was right about that.

'I'll go,' said Hope, hesitating to glance at

her phone, and then the hall, and then her phone again. 'Don't let that out of your sight, Mum.' She pointed to the phone before dashing to the front door.

It was a gloriously sunny morning and for a second, she was blinded by the rays as she opened the door, before being hit by the chilly air with added bite from a gusting wind.

'Good morning, Hope.'

'Laurence! Please don't tell me you've thought of another way to murder me. You have got to stop doing this.'

'Oh. Erm. No. I was on my way to The Royal Oak for a pint. Coffee not beer. And a hearty Full English breakfast. Writer's block is grim. I need to eat, drink, and people watch to get some inspiration.' He shook his head mournfully and let out a dramatic sigh. 'Anyway, as I was passing your house I just thought I'd check that everything's sorted for the book launch on Thursday.'

Hope frowned at him. 'You know it is. I confirmed it all the other day. It's hardly a major event and … Oh. I didn't mean it wasn't important. Or major in the publishing world. I meant in terms of what we needed to do to fulfil our brief. You're the most important part, so as long as you're there, it'll be brilliant.'

'Hmm. Nice try. Don't worry. I know

what you mean. Other than me, my books, my agent, a room full of chairs, and some tables for canapes and drinks, plus a couple of banners, there wasn't that much to do.' He grinned. 'I hope your invoice reflects that.'

'It will. But you forgot the window display, the A board outside, and the dramatic staging of the murderer's cloak and the murder weapon in front of the beautifully painted backdrop. If I could've got the small lake you wanted, and a doll that didn't make it look tacky, I would've done so. Do you want to come in?' She silently prayed that he would say no.

Her prayer was answered. 'Thanks, but I'm starving. I was up most of the night writing and then the last two hours – nothing. Not one word. And about that lake. I fully accept you were right. A child's plastic paddling pool filled with water and a doll drowning would've just been wrong. Getting Hanna Shaw to paint that backdrop of the lake, the stately home, and the Lady in the Lake's arm reaching out in vain as she sinks beneath the water was a master stroke of genius.'

'Thank you. I'm delighted I've made you happy.'

'You always make me happy, Hope. Erm. Would you like to join me for breakfast? My treat.'

'That's kind. But sadly I can't. We're so busy and I've got a jam-packed day ahead of me.'

'Rain check?'

'Absolutely. I hope the words come tumbling out after breakfast.'

'I hope so too. I've got a deadline looming. No pun intended.'

'Because you write cosy crime, you mean? Oh yes.'

'Hope? May I ask you something?'

A slight shiver ran up her spine. But that might've been from the chilly wind, not a premonition.

'Y-es.' She eyed him warily nonetheless.

'Would you read my manuscript when it's completed? I want you to be the first, as you're the heroine in my book.'

'Blimey, Laurence. But I thought you bump me off?'

He shook his head. 'So did I. But it seems I can't. I realised that last night. I want you to live, Hope. And I want you to be in my next book too. The one after this. In fact, I think I want to make you into a series.'

'Wow! I don't know what to say. The thing is, I don't get much time to read books.' His face fell so she quickly added, 'But if it's important to you then I'll certainly do my very best to find the time. It won't be finished for a while, will it?'

He brightened suddenly. 'Do you know what? I think it might. I've just had a flash of inspiration. I must dash off and get it written down before I lose my train of thought. You're my inspiration, Hope. My muse. Have a wonderful day.'

'Thank you,' she said, as Laurence rushed next door to the pub, his laptop in one hand as he waved to her with the other.

# Nine

Tuesday was a much better day than Monday. Not only had the Eversleys got their horse for Della Hardy, having tentatively agreed an exceptionally reasonable price with Griff's friend, Hope had found a troupe of male dancers who were more than willing to remove their clothes, as per Rita and Vera Boot's request. The roulette wheel and poker table were also in the bag, as Simon liked to say. And by the end of the day, Hope had solved the fairy grotto problem. Thanks in part to her conversation with Laurence that morning.

Hanna Shaw was a talented artist. She had performed a minor miracle at the Mistletoe Dance with her superb winter wonderland forest backdrop to the Christmas trees. The backdrop for Laurence's book launch was a work of art in every sense. A true trompe l'oeil that was both beautiful and yet mildly menacing, which was perfect for a cosy crime novel. A fairy grotto would be a breeze for her.

Hope could add living plants and flowers and perhaps a little waterfall, and although the paddling pool idea was inappropriate for Laurence's event, the one shaped like a lily pond that Hope had seen on line, might be just the thing for Della's.

Hanna lived in Catkin Cottage on Oak Street which was only round the corner from The White House, and Hope paid her a visit shortly before five p.m. to ask if Hanna could fit in a new commission and if she would be able to come up with something in time.

'I'd certainly be up for that,' Hanna said, inviting Hope in. 'What do you have in mind?'

Hope followed Hanna into the sitting room and sat on the sofa explaining Della's requirements in detail while Hanna opened a bottle of white wine, on the premise that it was always past six p.m. somewhere on the planet and that meant it was time for wine.

'A fairy grotto?' Hanna giggled, handing Hope a glass and sitting sideways on an armchair opposite, dangling her legs over the arm. 'How old is this client?'

'Thanks,' said Hope grateful that there were no events tonight, so in theory, no last-minute emergencies. 'Twenty, I believe. And if you could add a unicorn that would be the icing on the cake.'

'A unicorn?' Hanna shrugged. 'But of course. Every fairy grotto needs a unicorn. Sorry. I shouldn't make fun of people. I think it's lovely that this young woman wants something magical. It beats the plain old posh restaurant, champagne, and a ring in a glass, or a cake, I suppose.'

'Funnily enough I was only thinking the other day that I wished more people would go the restaurant route. It would make our lives sooooo much easier.' Hope laughed.

'But not as much fun or nearly as exciting. Cheers!'

'Cheers!' Hope raised her glass as had Hanna. 'Would you be able to let me have some sort of quick mock-up in a day or two so that I can run it by the client and her brother? Unfortunately I don't have the venue yet so I can't give you dimensions of where the fairy grotto will fit. Is that a problem at this stage?'

Hanna shook her head. 'Yes I can, and no it isn't.'

'Brilliant! You're the best, Hanna.'

'Valentine's Day must be difficult for you.'

Hope was taken aback by that comment. 'For me? Why?'

Hanna laughed. 'No need to look so surprised. I didn't mean you personally. I meant all the team at Eversley Events. You've always had events on that day, and sometimes several I believe. Do any of you ever get a chance to take that night off? Grace might find it a pain this year, now that's she with Griff.'

Hope relaxed. 'Oh I see. It hasn't really been an issue. Mum and Dad celebrate it either before or after the actual day. I can't remember the last time I wasn't single on the day so it's never affected me, and as Grace is moving in with Griff this week, I'm sure they'll manage to celebrate it somehow.'

'Grace is moving in with Griff? Wow. That's fast. But good for her.'

'Ah. I'm not sure I should've told you that. Please don't let on that you know.'

Hanna smiled. 'You can count on me to keep quiet.' She eyed Hope over the rim of her glass. 'Not tempted to join her at the big house?'

Hope rolled her eyes. 'I assume you're referring to Russell. The answer would be no. I think he's great. I really do. But I just don't love him. I must admit though, it might start to feel weird from now on. My sister's going to be living with Griff, my best friend will soon be married, and her sister's now with the man of her dreams. So that leaves me on my lonesome.'

'Oh yeah! I heard about Naomi and

Lucas and I was lucky enough to meet him yesterday. Only briefly. They were in the pub last night. I can definitely see why Naomi wanted to find him.'

'I haven't met him yet. Grace has. She also said he's lovely. Fi invited us to her parents' for a quick drink on Friday before they all head off to Folkestone for the family celebration, so I'll meet him then.'

'What's with that? I mean who wants a massive family gathering and a huge meal the night before their wedding? I know I shouldn't say this but Greg's family seems a little odd to me.'

Hope nodded. 'They're definitely ... different. And I'm with you on the meal, but Fi adores him and she'll do anything that makes him happy. He feels the same about her, so that's fair enough.'

'I don't know him that well but I've always thought Greg was ... a little boring. Nice to look at but I feel I want to find his 'go faster button' and give it an almighty push.'

'Me too,' admitted Hope. 'I've asked Fi a million times what it is that makes her love him. All she says is he has that special something. I have no idea what that is. Grace says she knows. Not about Greg but about Griff. She says he's got that special something too and that when I meet the right one for me, I'll know exactly what it is.'

'Fair point. I can see that. I guess it's a sort of beauty is in the eye of the beholder kind of thing.'

'Except it's not about looks, according to Mum, Grace, and Fi. It's about a feeling. About just knowing that he's the one for you and it's meant to be.'

'Hmm. You ever felt that?'

Hope took a large gulp of wine. 'I thought I had once. I was wrong. Now I'm not sure. Although... no. I'm not sure. What about you?'

Hanna shook her head. 'Nope. Never. Here's to us singletons.'

Hope raised her glass again and they toasted to being single.

But secretly, if Hope had her way and a certain someone was as nice in the flesh as he sounded on the phone, there was a chance, however slight, that she might not be single for that much longer.

Although as he lived in Bournemouth and she lived in Betancourt Bay, how that would work was a mystery.

# Ten

Hope had only intended to have one glass of wine at Hanna's but before she knew it, Hanna had opened a second bottle.

'I must go,' Hope said half an hour later, getting up from the sofa with some difficulty. 'Thank you so much for this evening. It's been great fun.'

'It has. We must do it again very soon. You're welcome anytime. I'll be in touch in a day or two with a rough sketch of the fairy grotto.'

'Perfect,' Hope said stumbling towards the front door.

The cold evening air slammed into her the moment she stepped outside taking her breath away momentarily and making her gasp. She wrapped her scarf tighter around her neck and walked as fast as she could.

When the door of The Royal Oak opened and she heard her name, she didn't bother to lift her head to see who had called her.

'Not tonight, Laurence,' she called back. She was more than a little annoyed when she heard the footfall right behind her and was tempted to punch him on the nose once again. This time on purpose.

'It's not Laurence,' Russell Betancourt said. 'I haven't seen you for a while. How are you, Hope?'

She cast her startled eyes on his handsome face. Why couldn't she fall in love with him? Life would be so much simpler.

'Freezing,' she said. 'You?'

He took off his coat and she gasped as he went to wrap it around her shoulders.

'I've been okay. I don't suppose you fancy joining me for a drink in the pub do you?'

'Thanks for the coat, Russell, but please put it back on. I'm almost home and you'll freeze to death.' She handed it back to him and he shrugged. 'And thanks for the offer, but unfortunately I've had more than I should have at Hanna's.' He looked deflated. 'Maybe another time?'

He brightened visibly. 'Absolutely. Whenever. Just say the word.' He fell into step beside her. 'Other than freezing, you've been okay?'

Hope nodded. 'Yeah. Rushed off my feet as usual, but you know what that's like.'

He shook his head. 'Not really. The

auction house runs like a finely tuned machine, and Betancourt does the same, now that Griff's taken over from Dad. That's not official yet, but we all know it's for the best. And, of course, you know that Bianca has finally moved on. That's a huge relief to us all. There's a warning there. Don't marry in haste.'

'Don't marry at all.' Hope laughed.

'You don't … you don't mean that, do you? You want a family and children, don't you?'

'Right now, all I want is a roaring fire, a hot cup of tea, and a chance to put my feet up.' She stopped at her front door and turned to face him. He deserved an answer. 'Other than that, I'm not sure what I want. I've always assumed that one day I'll meet someone and fall in love, and that if it's meant to be, kids will come along after that. But the truth is, none of us has a clue what the future holds. I do know what it doesn't. I care about you, Russell, you know that. And because I do, I need to be honest with you. I thought you understood at Christmas. Perhaps I didn't explain myself properly. We'll always be friends. We'll never be more than that. I'm truly sorry. I wish I could give you hope.' She gave a mirthless laugh. 'In every sense. But I can't. I won't change my mind. We've known one another far too long to pretend things could be otherwise. There's someone out there for you, Russell. Someone who will love you as you deserve to be loved. That someone is not me.'

He had held her gaze throughout, but now he stared at his shoes.

'I'm sorry,' she added, her heart almost breaking for him. 'More than you know.'

He nodded slowly, lifted his head, raked a hand through his thick, blond hair, and gave her a half smile. Sadness filled his eyes when he spoke.

'I know, Hope. I think I've always known. But just for a minute, for one tiny moment, I wanted to believe that it could be you. I know you won't change your mind.' He gave a strangled laugh. 'I've known you long enough to know that once you make your mind up about something, nothing will change it. But if you ever want anything, or need my help in any way, just ask. You'll always have my friendship.' He swallowed hard. 'And my love.'

She stood on her tiptoes, grabbed the collar of his shirt, pulled him towards her, and planted a kiss on his cheek. 'And you'll always have mine.'

He sucked in a breath and looked her in the eye. 'Goodnight, Hope,' he said, his voice cracking with emotion. And then he turned and marched away.

Tears pricked her eyes as she shoved open the front door and stepped inside. She closed it behind her and fell back against it, exhaling a long and laboured breath.

Why was Love so unfair? Why couldn't she have simply loved him?

'Is that you, Hope?' Grace called from upstairs. 'Will you give me a hand with my packing? Griff's coming here tomorrow to help me move and I don't know where to start.'

Hope swallowed hard and swiped at her eyes, coughing before she replied. 'I'm just going to take Lady E for a walk and then I'll help. You're only taking your clothes and personal belongings so it won't take long.'

She couldn't face Grace right now. She couldn't listen to her sister's excitement, after breaking Russell's heart. She needed to be alone.

And Lady E, having heard her name and the word 'walk' in the same sentence, was already scurrying down the hall, her little stubby tail wagging, and her big bat ears flapping as she ran.

Hope swept the dog up in her arms and gave her a kiss and a cuddle, and then she attached the lead and ventured back out into the cold night air.

Lady E trotted along beside her as she took the long way round to the beach thus avoiding the need to pass Laurence's cottage. She certainly wasn't in the mood for him tonight. This route took an extra fifteen minutes to reach the sands below but it was worth it.

The tide was low, like yesterday, and the waves rolled gently in, and swished and swashed back out over the ripples on the sand. The almost full moon hung over the horizon like a huge beach ball, the reflection bouncing over the dark waters of the English Channel and onto the sand stretched out before her. She would check the forecast on her phone before she let Lady E off the lead tonight.

That's when she saw the missed call.

'Damn. Damn. Damn.' Tom Hardy had called her while she was at Hanna's and she'd missed it.

It must've been when she'd gone upstairs to the loo. As she was coming out of the bathroom she'd spotted a painting Hanna was working on and she'd cheekily poked her head into the spare room that Hanna used as her studio due to it being north facing, in order to get a better look. She had then called down to Hanna and told her what she was doing, and Hanna had come up to tell her more about it.

'It's the Mistletoe Dance, isn't it?' Hope said, and Hanna nodded. 'And is that Grace and Griff taking centre stage on the dance floor?'

'It is. It's almost finished but there's just something missing and I'm not sure what that is yet.' Hanna tilted her head from side to side and Hope did likewise. 'I don't know what made me decide to paint it, or to make it life-size, but I sat down and did a sketch and then I realised what I wanted, and this is what appeared.'

'It's breathtakingly beautiful, Hanna. It really is. I think it's perfect as it is. But you're the artist so what do I know? There's an ethereal quality about it. This is exactly the sort of thing I'm imagining for the fairy grotto.'

'Yeah. It would definitely work for that.'

'It's exquisite. It's almost as if only Grace and Griff are in the present in the room and everyone else is from another time or place. They're not ghostly but they don't seem to be of this world. Does that make sense?'

Hanna beamed at her. 'That's precisely what I was going for. I remember watching them that night and they were mesmerising. I can't explain it but the love they felt for each other seemed to shine out from them as they danced.'

'It shines out from this painting. Do you … do you intend to sell it?'

Hanna met her gaze and shrugged. 'I

hadn't thought that far ahead. But yes. I suppose so. Do you think they might want to buy it?'

'Absolutely! But I've got something else in mind for it first. Do you think it'll be finished by not this Saturday but the one after?'

'It could be. Why? What's happening that day?'

'I'm sworn to secrecy, I'm afraid, but let's just say this painting would be perfect.'

'Then yes. It'll be ready by the Friday night before.'

Hope might've missed Tom's call, but it was worth it.

She checked her watch and rang him back.

His laughter greeted her but it sounded as if he was jumping up and down. 'This is becoming a habit. Although it's not as late as yesterday. I did call earlier.'

Hope laughed too. 'I know. I saw the missed call. Sorry about that. I was with an artist sorting out some pieces.'

'No problem. How was your day?'

'Strange. Emotional. Good. Yours?'

He laughed louder. 'Strange. Unemotional. Not bad.'

'I have good news.'

'Excellent.' He breathed hard.

'Am I interrupting something? Only it

sounds as if you're bouncing up and down. Or having ... Oh! You're not...?'

Hope flushed red at the thought and he laughed even harder.

'I wish! Do you seriously think I'd be talking to you if I were?'

'I hope not. But hey. Whatever floats your boat.'

'I'm running. And it's along a sandy beach right now. But I'll stop and walk so that we can talk.'

'I won't keep you long then.'

'You can keep me as long as you want, Hope.'

God! His voice was so sexy.

'Right. Erm. We've got the horse. A mare called Brilliant Day and she is absolutely stunning. I'll text you a photo. Hold on.' She sent the photo Grace had sent to Pat, who had forwarded it to Hope's phone. 'The price is really good but let me know if it's a problem.'

'It won't be. And you're right. She is beautiful.'

'As for the fairy grotto. The artist I mentioned will be painting a trompe l'oeil backdrop and we'll add fresh flowers, plants, and maybe even a few small blossom trees if we can find some ready to flower. She'll have something to show me in a day or two and I'll send it to you and to Della, if that's okay.

Then you and she can liaise and get back to me with any comments or changes.'

'I have a comment now,' he teased, the laughter evident in his tone. 'You're incredible, Hope. I'm impressed.'

'Didn't you think you would be?'

'Truthfully? I wasn't one hundred per cent sure.'

'Well I'm just happy we could help.'

'Not as happy as I am. Or as Della will be. You do know she'll want to buy this horse, don't you?'

'Sadly, she's not for sale. The fairy grotto backdrop may be though, if Della likes it.'

'How big will it be?'

'I'm not sure yet. That'll depend on the venue, and we haven't found that yet. Now I've gone down in your estimation, haven't I?'

'I don't think that's possible. But are you saying you've got the horse and the fairy grotto but nowhere for Della to propose?'

'Not yet. Don't worry. I'll find somewhere. Leave it with me. Erm. Do you know when you'll be arriving in Folkestone?'

'I'm already here. I arrived tonight. That's why I'm out running. I've been sitting in the car for hours. The traffic was a nightmare. I need to run again for a little while but don't hang up. We can still talk.'

It took Hope a moment to take that in.

'You're here? In Folkestone?'

She looked westward towards Folkestone and could see the Harbour Arm from where she stood. To think that Tom was somewhere on that beach just a mile or two away. That sent all sorts of tingles and shivers and hot flushes shooting around her body like a box of fireworks dropped into a fire.

And then her heart almost stopped.

She tingled with excitement as she spotted the tall, tanned, athletic, blond-haired figure running towards her from the west and her smile was as broad as the English Channel by the time he was close enough for her to wave at him.

But Lady E reached him first and she almost tripped him up as she danced up and down in front of him on her hind legs. Hope felt like doing the same.

The stranger stopped briefly, bent forward, and tickled Lady E's big bat-like ears, before continuing on his way, and now he was even closer.

'I think I can see you,' she whispered down the phone, her voice husky and seductive.

'You can? How? Where are you?' His voice matched hers, although his breathlessness could've also been due to the fact he was running.

'I'm on the beach at the foot of the cliffs in Betancourt Bay.' She could hardly contain her excitement now.

'Erm. Betancourt Bay?' He sounded disappointed. 'Then whoever it is you're looking at is not me. I'm just about to reach the Harbour Arm in Folkestone. I wish it was me though. I'd love to see you tonight.'

'Me too,' said Hope, staring at the runner who was now waving back at her and closing the distance between them in record time that would make an Olympic Gold medal sprinter look sluggish.

Hope gulped in surprise and her eyes opened wide as realisation dawned.

'I'm sorry, Tom. I have to go. But I'll call you first thing tomorrow.'

'Erm. Okay. Goodnight, Hope.'

'Goodnight, Tom.'

The runner was now just a few feet from her and the man was no stranger. But he had changed so much since the last time she had seen him that she hadn't recognised him until just a moment ago.

It was her ex-boyfriend, Rob.

And he was looking better than he ever had when they were dating.

# Eleven

'Hello Hope,' he said, smiling broadly. 'I was planning to come and see you soon but this is even better. I always wonder if I might bump into you on one of my visits home, but I didn't expect to see you on this beach at this time of night. I assume that is your dog. So how have you been?'

Hope finally found her voice. 'How … how have I been? Are you being serious? It's been eight years, Rob.'

He had broken her heart at university, when he'd told her he would not be returning to Betancourt Bay, but was instead going to travel the world for a year or two, working as he went to support himself and to enable him to move on to the next destination. That was eight years ago.

Hope was fully aware that he had been back a few times since to visit his parents, Jean and Victor Mills who lived in Rosehip Cottage, but those visits had been fleeting and he'd never once made time to knock on the front door of The White House and say hello to her.

A tiny furrow formed between his brows. 'Eight years? Yes, I suppose it has. But it doesn't feel that long.'

Hope wanted to scream, 'It does to me!' Instead she said, 'Time flies when you're having fun.'

He tilted his head to one side. 'You or me? It hasn't all been fun, you know. I've had to work along the way. There've been one or two close shaves with dangerous creatures, both animal and human. And I've missed you, Hope. More than I thought I would. I must say, you're looking stunning. If I'd known you'd look this good I would've come home sooner. That was a joke. You always looked good. I've wanted to come to your house so many times over the years, Hope. But I knew I couldn't. If I saw you again I knew I'd want to stay and I couldn't do that to myself. I needed to get the wanderlust out of my system before I could think of settling down. I hope you understand that. But God I've thought of you so often. I can't believe it's eight years and I still haven't got over you.' He looked her in the eye. 'What about you, Hope? Have you got over me?'

He moved closer and slipped a hand around her waist, easing her towards him until their faces almost touched.

Why couldn't she speak? Why couldn't she push him away?

'No. Not entirely,' she whispered.

Why hadn't she lied?

The smile spread across his face and he tilted her chin upwards with one finger of his free hand then he traced a line from her chin to her lips, across her left cheek and then down to her neck.

'You have no idea how happy that makes me,' he said, his voice thick with pent up desire.

'Rob,' she said. 'It's been eight years.' She had meant to chastise him but it had sounded more like a plea, even to her ears. What on earth was wrong with her?

'Don't worry. I'll be gentle. We can make up for lost time, Hope, and we've got the rest of our lives ahead of us.'

His lips came down on hers and the kiss was intense. At least on his part. He kissed her hard and held her so tight that she felt her bones might break. If this was gentle, she wouldn't want to experience the opposite.

'God, Hope,' he groaned as he slid his lips across her mouth. 'You can still turn me on in a split second. I want you so much, it hurts.' And then he kissed her again in a way that made it clear he was hoping for a great deal more than kissing.

# Twelve

After her encounter with Rob, Hope had gone to bed the moment she got home. But she hadn't slept at all and spent the night tossing and turning, flitting between feelings of anger, surprise, a strange sort of guilt, an odd type of happiness, but mostly just doubt, concern and incredulity.

She spent the whole of Wednesday in a sort of dream. No. Not a dream. More of a twilight zone. She felt zombified. As if she wasn't quite sure who she was, where she was, or what she wanted.

Her family spent the entire day asking if she was coming down with something.

'What happened with you last night?' Grace asked at breakfast. 'You said you'd help me pack. If Mum hadn't stepped in, I'd be buried under a pile of clothes this morning.' Grace gave her a playful nudge. 'Everything okay, Hope? You look shattered.'

Hope nodded. 'Sorry. Felt tired. Went to

bed.'

'Are you unwell, darling?' Pat asked her eyes filled with concern as she poured Hope a large cup of coffee.

'No. I don't know. Maybe,' Hope said.

'You do look a bit drained today, sweetheart,' said Simon. 'You've had a lot going on. We all have. But maybe this new client is the straw that broke the camel's back.'

'No! Not him. I mean her. Them. Whatever. It's not that.'

Grace chuckled. 'Dad just called you a camel and you didn't come back with a retort. You must be ill. Quick. Call the vet.'

'It's those late night walks on the beach,' said Granny Joy. 'Or your love life.'

'Love life?' queried Grace. 'What love life? Do you know something I don't?' Grace glanced from one to another of her family and gave Hope a second nudge. 'Are you keeping secrets, Hope?'

'Yes. No. Erm. Look. I'm just ... not feeling quite right today. Can you all give me a break, please?'

'Sorry,' said Grace.

'Take things easy today, darling,' said Pat.

'We can deal with everything today,' said Simon. 'You get some rest.'

'I'm moving out this morning, don't

forget,' said Grace. 'I thought we could all go out tonight to celebrate my new life, as we don't have any actual events happening this evening. But we can do that another night if you're not feeling up to it, Hope.'

'No. It's fine. I'll be okay. Although it might be better another night. We've all got a lot going on this week. It's going to be strange you not being here though. Weird.' Hope let out a sigh. 'I'm ... I'm going to miss you.'

Grace laughed. 'I'll be right across the road. Not in the back of beyond.' She wrapped an arm around Hope's shoulder. 'But I know what you mean. I'll miss you too. All of you. I'll miss these breakfasts. I'll miss Lady E. I'll have to come back and have sleepovers every so often. How about that?'

'That would be lovely,' said Pat.

'If you can drag yourself away from Grifforde,' said Granny Joy. 'I know where I'd rather spend the night. Every night. And it isn't here. If I were a few years younger, you'd have some serious competition for that man.'

Grace pulled a face. 'You've got a point. Maybe I'll just come over for breakfast. Or lunch. Or dinner.'

'This will always be your home as far as your dad and I are concerned and you'll always be welcome,' Pat said, her voice filled with emotion.

'Thanks, Mum. I'll be able to say I'm someone with two homes.' Grace joked.

'Oh. I almost forgot, Hope,' said Simon. 'I bumped into Laurence Lake this morning on Lady E's walk. He asked me to tell you that he's almost finished the new book and he can't wait for you to read it. He's hoping to give it to you tomorrow night at his book launch. I hope you'll be well enough to attend that. But if you're not, one of us will go. I know he'll understand.'

'What's this?' Grace asked. 'Why's he giving you his new book to read? Oh. It's because you're the main character in this one, aren't you?'

The last thing Hope wanted to think about right now was Laurence Lake. Or his new book. As for reading the damn thing, she really wasn't in the mood for finding out all the different ways he had thought up to try to murder her.

Although on second thought, death might not be so bad.

# Thirteen

This evening was the book launch for The Lady in the Lake, Laurence Lake's newest publication. Hope had been the one who had organised this event so she could hardly ask one of the others to cover it, as tempting as it was to pull a sicky and stay at home, far from his murderous ways, and out of sight of the rest of the world.

She had done that yesterday. In fact, other than her family, and Griff who had come to help Grace move to Betancourt, Hope hadn't seen another person throughout the entire day.

Not Rob, who had tried to call her several times and who she had finally texted back to say she was unbelievably busy and she'd get back to him soon.

None of her clients. Thankfully no one had called with a dire emergency, although several people had phoned her to chat about other things, and one or two, to change some minor details regarding their particular event.

And sadly, not Tom Hardy. They kept missing one another's calls. He had called her early in the morning, when she had been in the shower. She called him back as soon as she saw the missed call, and got his voicemail.

She missed his second call when the entire family were on the doorstep of The White House seeing Grace off to her new home.

'We're only across the road,' said Griff, clearly thinking it might be a little over the top for the family to feel the need to wave Grace off, especially as she only had two suitcases, a handbag, and her laptop bag. 'You're all welcome at Betancourt. Pop in whenever you want, day or night. Our home is yours.'

That had only made Pat more emotional and she hugged Grace even tighter.

'You're starting a whole new life, darling and you're going to be so happy.'

Hope had tutted. 'And that's why you're crying, is it? You weren't this tearful when I went off to uni and that was hundreds of miles away.'

'Because we knew you'd be coming back one day,' said Simon. 'Grace is leaving home for good.'

Hope pulled a face. 'Thanks. I think.'

But even she felt emotional as she gave her sister a hug. 'You take care of her,' she said to Griff, knowing that he would.

She felt even more emotional when she saw she'd missed that second call from Tom. And rather annoyed when yet again, she got his voicemail. But they were both busy people with businesses to run so she knew it wasn't his fault. Or hers. Although now that he was just a stone's throw away with his sister and her girlfriend in Folkestone, Hope was anxious to set a date and time to meet.

She was helping Granny Joy take a mid-morning shower when she missed the third call from Tom. Granny Joy had somehow managed to get herself covered from head to toe in flour and some unknown sticky substance that looked worryingly like treacle mixed with chocolate spread. Hope had been working in the sitting room and had put her phone on charge when she heard her mum's shriek. She ran into the kitchen and saw Granny Joy covered in brown goo.

'What have you done?' Pat cried. 'I've got a client to meet in half an hour!'

'I'll sort it out, Mum,' Hope had said. 'Don't worry. You go to your meeting. Leave Granny Joy to me.'

She had forgotten about her phone in all the commotion that followed.

Granny Joy insisted she didn't need a shower when Hope told her she did.

'I had one this morning.'

'And now you need another.' Hope edged her forward.

Granny Joy dug her heels in and folded her arms across her chest.

'Why? All I've been doing is baking cakes. How dirty can a person get baking cakes?'

'A person? Not very. You, it seems, exceedingly. Come along, Granny Joy.' Hope took her hand and led her towards the kitchen door.

Granny Joy pulled back and pointed. 'But I've just put a cake in the oven. I can't leave it.'

Hope let out a sigh and wrapped an arm around Granny Joy's shoulder. 'Yes you can. And that's the fridge, not the oven.'

'I wondered why the damn thing wasn't getting hot. Who moved the oven?'

'This isn't your kitchen, so the oven is in a different place to where it is at your house.'

'Then take me home and I'll put it in my own oven.'

'Okey dokey. You come along with me then but how about we take a little shower first?'

'Oh, all right. But you're not getting in the shower with me. You can use your own shower.'

It wasn't until half an hour later that Hope finally returned to the sitting room, Simon having taken over care of Granny Joy.

Hope saw Tom's missed call and called him back but it had gone to voicemail. He'd called her again much later, and this time she was taking a relaxing bath. Staying at home and trying to make sense of your life, and sort out other people's was extremely tiring and she had hoped a soothing bath before supper, listening to her favourite music, might help. Her phone was on her bed and when she heard it ring, she had tried to climb out and get to it but she had slipped and fallen on the floor. Luckily she wasn't hurt, but by the time she got up and grabbed the phone, he had rung off and left a message.

'Hello Hope. It seems we aren't meant to talk today,' he said, his voice a mixture of humour and disappointment. 'I'm about to meet Alice's family. Alice is Della's girlfriend. But I expect you know that. Anyway, I thought it was just drinks and dinner but it seems it's going to be a long night, so I don't think I'll be able to call you later. I hope you're okay. Please leave me a message if you can. Just to let me know you're fine. Hopefully we'll speak tomorrow, and I'll … we'll see you soon. Have a lovely evening.'

She quickly called him back but again it

went to voicemail. She left him a message.

'Hi Tom. Have a good time tonight. Please say hello to Della for me. And Alice. I'm fine thanks, but it's been a strange day. I'm looking forward to meeting you though. Erm. I've got meetings all day tomorrow, and an event I can't get out of in the evening. Friday's jam-packed with another event in the evening. Again, one I can't get out of. A wedding on Saturday that's both business and pleasure, so I've got to be there, and an eightieth birthday party on Sunday that I definitely need to attend, partly to ensure the police aren't called.' She laughed. 'I'll explain when we talk. Erm. Monday evening is free. If that works for you. And for Della of course. Sorry I can't do anything before then. But I will get the sketch of the fairy grotto to you tomorrow and I'll also update you on the venue situation. It'll all be fine, so don't worry. Speak soon.'

Her phone rang a second after she'd hung up and she was so certain it was Tom, she didn't check.

'I was hoping you'd call back,' she said, unable to contain her joy.

'Oh! That's good to hear,' said Laurence. 'But what do you mean, call back?'

'Oh,' she said completely downhearted. 'It's you. I was hoping it was someone else.'

'Thank you very much!'

'Sorry, Laurence. Don't take it personally. How can I help you?'

'Fine. I was just checking if Simon gave you my message. It's almost done, Hope. And I'm dying to know what you think of it.'

'The new book, you mean? Dad did. But as I said the other day, I'm really busy at the moment so I'm not sure when I'll get a chance to read it.'

'Take it to bed with you,' he said.

'I go to bed to sleep, Laurence.'

'Ah, Hope,' he said, a hint of teasing in his tone. 'That's something we need to work on.'

'Is it? I'm fine with things the way they are, thanks. I think Mum needs me so I've got to go. I'll see you tomorrow evening.'

'Oh. Okay. Don't be late.'

'I'll be early. Bye Laurence.' She rang off before he could say anything further.

It wasn't that she didn't like him, because she did. But what he'd said to her on Tuesday morning on the doorstep of The White House had unnerved her. And that comment just now about her sleeping hadn't helped. She thought of him as a friend but there was something in the way he'd looked at her on Tuesday morning that had made her think he might be starting to see her as something else.

He'd said she was his inspiration and his

muse. That might've just been writer's talk, and might mean nothing, but she couldn't shake the feeling that he had meant it as something more. Something ... special.

She sincerely hoped she was wrong.

Having one man in the village declaring his love for her had been bad enough. Although since their heart-to-heart, Russell Betancourt had returned to London telling his family that he might not be back for a while.

Perhaps that was what he needed to do to get over her. She could only hope it would work. For his sake as well as hers. And she wished him well.

Having two men in love with her was a real problem, assuming Rob had been sincere on Tuesday night. She had no reason to think he wasn't, even if he hadn't been in touch with her for the past eight years, or even attempted to see her when he'd come home.

He had explained that. And she believed him.

She also had to admit that something had sparked inside her when he'd kissed her. Not a flame exactly; more of a flicker. A tiny spark. A memory of what there had once been. Could they ever get back all that they had lost?

He wasn't happy that she had eventually

demanded he stop. His hands were about to explore her body, his fingers just an inch from her breast and it had taken all her strength, both physical and mental, to push him away.

Were the feelings he had aroused in her, for him? Or was it simply that it had been so long since she had slept with anyone, that her body was merely reacting to a man's touch? Just responding to the signals?

Having three men in love with her was just ridiculous. She was no beauty. She had a good figure but certainly not one that would make every man fall at her feet.

And yet she had an awful feeling that Laurence Lake felt more for her than friendship. She would need to nip that in the bud before he got any ideas. It had been so hard letting Russell down. The thought of doing that again to someone else filled her heart with sadness.

And then there was Tom Hardy. The one man she actually thought she might have genuine feelings for, and she hadn't even met him. How ludicrous was that? Could you fall for someone you've never met? What if he looked like a frog? Would a kiss make her believe he was a prince?

And why, if she did have feelings for Tom, had she let Rob kiss her? Was it down to shock. The shock of seeing him again after all those years. Especially as he looked so good. Or the shock of the things he said. More likely it was thanks to drinking too much wine with Hanna earlier in the evening. And on an empty stomach.

Rob had said he would call her the following day, and he had, but Hope had told him she was busy. That wasn't a lie. She had so much to do and so many events that she didn't have time for men. Any man.

Apart from Tom Hardy, perhaps.

Today she must concentrate on Laurence Lake. One hundred and fifty people were attending this launch and it had to be a success. Not just because Laurence and his publishers were clients, but because he was a friend. A friend and nothing more though, as she might need to remind him.

Hope had considered inviting Tom, and possibly even Della, to this event, but as it was ticket-only, and she had no idea if either of them knew who Laurence Lake was, or if they read his books, she thought better of it.

Not only that, but the event was completely sold out within a week of it being announced. She knew that Laurence was a successful author, but she had no idea quite how popular he was.

That was something that was brought home to her when she arrived at Bishop's Books just after four p.m. that afternoon. A queue had formed outside and was already snaking along the road in front of several other shops, including Greg Bishop's uncle's estate agency in which a large poster had been placed with a big red arrow drawn onto it, pointing to the bookshop. The poster was now hidden from view by the crowds of people standing in line, as was the window display in the bookshop itself, and the A board outside.

Fortunately, Hope, along with the team who would help set things up and were hired to do all the heavy lifting, would be entering via the rear thus avoiding the crowds altogether.

'Blimey,' Hope said, once she was inside Bishop's Books. 'I hadn't expected that.'

Greg Bishop smiled. 'The queue? Because you didn't realise Laurence and his books are loved by so many people?'

Hope smiled back. 'No. Well, yes. But mainly because it's only four, and the event doesn't start for another two hours.'

Greg laughed. 'That's not the best bit.' He nodded his head towards the pavement. 'Those people in the queue don't have tickets.'

'What!' Hope couldn't believe her ears, and she turned to look at the queue once more. 'None of them?'

Greg shook his head. 'Not one.'

'How do you know that?'

'Because I asked them.'

'When did they start arriving?'

'The shop was getting busy from about two this afternoon. A few people purchased books and then left, but I noticed that several people seemed to be lingering. When I asked if I could help them find what they were looking for, I realised most of them were here in the hope of seeing Laurence. Once the shop started getting packed, I had no choice but to tell everyone that they had to purchase something or leave as we were organising an event and would be closing in order to set that up. That was around three thirty. It took me fifteen minutes to usher everyone outside and although I told them there were no tickets left and that they wouldn't be able to see the author, there they all are. The queue gets longer every minute, it seems.'

'I hope the sales of Laurence's books make up for your lost profit.'

Greg's smile grew wider. 'Oh they will, believe me. And the best thing about these events is the attendees often buy other books as well. Not just earlier books by Laurence they might have missed but also books by other authors. I'm planning to let them wander around the shop while Laurence does the signings. And if I know him well, which I do, he'll make his way outside at some stage to meet some of his other fans, and he'll probably persuade me to open up for anyone wanting to buy one of his books.'

'A win-win then. You'll be making money not just from those with tickets, but also from those without. What's your bestselling genre?' Hope glanced around the packed shelves filled with books from floor to ceiling.

'Apart from cosy crime, it has to be romance, and fantasy fiction. This shop stocks the largest number of fantasy fiction titles in the entire south east of England. It's my own personal favourite.' He leant forward conspiratorially. 'But don't tell Laurence I said that.'

Hope smiled. 'My lips are sealed. I'd better get to work.'

She walked towards the rear of the shop once again and to the large room at the back where the book launch was taking place. It was the only area in the premises that was large enough to fit in all the chairs, the trellis tables for the buffet food, and the staging required for the launch which was due to start at six p.m. sharp.

Laurence would be arriving around five and ticket holders would be let in from five thirty to give everyone time to take their seats before Laurence started his reading. But given the large queue outside, Hope might suggest having a couple of people standing at the doors to make way for the ticket holders. She'd chat with Greg and Laurence and his agent about that. Two of the guys who were helping set up the backdrop and the furniture would be more than happy to do that as it would mean extra money for them.

She gave instructions as to where the chairs and tables should be set up and where the backdrop should be positioned. She wanted Hanna's beautiful but menacing trompe l'oeil of the lake, the stately home, and the Lady in the Lake's arm reaching out in vain as she sinks beneath the water, to be visible from all angles, together with the dramatic staging of the murderer's cloak and the murder weapon in front of the incredible backdrop, and the room was big enough to allow for that.

The banners didn't take long to hang and the chairs and tables were all in place in plenty of time. The food arrived along with the bottles of wine and soft drinks shortly before the man himself, Laurence Lake, who declared he was thrilled and that Hope was a goddess.

'I'm delighted you're happy with it all,' she said. 'Are you nervous about your reading?'

'Not in the least. What I am nervous

about, is you.'

'Me? Why?'

'Because I've finished my new book and it's ready to receive your stamp of approval. Please be kind.'

He opened his tan leather briefcase and handed her a manuscript tied with a gold ribbon into which a single but exquisite red rose had been placed. The words, Destroying Angel by Laurence Lake were visible together with a hand written note that said, 'For Hope. My inspiration and my muse.'

'Oh! I assumed it would be a digital version.'

He raised his brows. 'Digital? You disappoint me, Hope, and I never thought I'd say those words about you. But never mind. I know exactly why you said it. Because you want to be able to carry it around with you and read it whenever and wherever you can. So just for you, and just this once, I'll send you a digital version by email. Give me five minutes.' He took the manuscript from her, removed the rose and handed that to her. 'A rose for a rose. I've had the thorns removed.' Then he took out his laptop and a few moments later, Hope's email on her phone pinged. 'Check it's there and you can open it,' he said. 'It's a PDF. I know you said you weren't an avid reader so I thought that might be the best format for you.'

She checked, and confirmed it was fine. 'Got it, thanks.'

'Excellent,' he said, taking her arm and leading her to one side. 'I meant what I said about you being my inspiration, Hope. My muse. And I'm dedicating this new book to you, as per the hand written note you saw. I would very much like to say something else, but this may not be the time or the place. Are you free for a drink afterwards? Just the two of us, somewhere quiet. Perhaps my cottage?'

'Oh!' She seemed to be saying that little word quite a lot recently. 'I'm happy to discuss anything you might want to say to me here, Laurence. We don't need somewhere quiet.'

Disappointment flickered in his eyes, but he took a deep breath and squeezed her arm a little tighter.

'Very well. I told you that you no longer die in this book because I want you to live, and I want you in my next book, and the book after that. I said I might make this a series, and I have decided I shall. And that's when it hit me. The reason I want you to live. The reason I want you in more books. The reason I had to write a love scene between the character based on you and the character based on me ... well not just one love scene, two or three, and one that is quite explicit, which is a first for me and may be a bit too raunchy for a cosy crime, but I was so excited I couldn't stop. And I'm waffling now. The reason for all of this is that I've fallen for you, Hope. I realise this may come as a surprise. It surprised me. But I think I love you.'

She almost burst out laughing – except it wasn't funny. It wasn't funny at all. And nor was the fact that he'd written a sex scene involving him and her. Precisely what she had been dreading might happen, had happened.

But why on earth would he pour out his heart to her here, at his book launch, shortly before he had an audience of his avid fans to please? Why hadn't he waited and picked the right moment?

Had it even occurred to him that she might not be pleased to receive his news? Was he so sure of himself and his charms that he thought he only had to tell her how he felt and she'd fall at his feet? What was it with some men that made them so sure women would love them, regardless of what they said or did?

'I don't know what to say.'

'It's a lot to take in,' he said, smiling at her.

'Yes.' She cleared her throat and stepped back an inch or two. 'The thing is, Laurence, I don't think you do. I think you have fallen for my character. And as we discussed the other day, I am nothing like her. I don't forage for mushrooms, or anything else in the woods. And, as thrilling as I'm sure your love scenes are, you and I won't be having sex. Not now or in the future. Plus, I don't read books. You were disappointed just now and that is because the person you've built me up to be in your mind and in your book, is not me. Not the real me, Laurence. You've turned me into something, or someone, you could fall in love with, but you haven't fallen in love with the real Hope Eversley. I know you'll see I'm right when you've had time to think about it. Time away from the character you've had in your head and heart for the last few months will help. But thank you for the compliment. Now I hate to cut this short but we do have an event starting very soon and we both need to be at our best for that. Give what I've said some thought, but you must excuse me for now.'

He stood blinking at her for a few moments and then he stepped aside to let her pass.

'I'll give it some thought,' he said, looking utterly bewildered. Perhaps she was the first woman to tell him she wasn't interested.

She was worried that this somewhat embarrassing episode might have a detrimental effect on the evening and for a while Laurence did seem unlike himself. But as soon as his fans began arriving, he was the Laurence Lake she knew and loved.

Well, not loved, but liked a lot as a friend. She hoped he would soon feel the same about her once more and forget this silly love nonsense. Only time would tell.

Once Laurence was in full flow, Hope took the opportunity to call Tom. He had left her a message earlier in the day to say that although he was disappointed that she couldn't make it sooner, Monday worked for him and Della and they were both excited to meet her. She hadn't had a chance to get back to him until now.

She asked Greg Bishop if she could go into the bookshop to make a call and he said that was fine.

'I've pulled down the blinds at the windows so that the fans still queuing outside have no inkling of what might be going on inside, and only a couple of wall lamps have been left on. It might be a bit gloomy in there. Turn on the lights if you want.'

'It'll be fine, thanks. And we don't want the fans outside to think you might be opening the shop back up.'

The shop wasn't gloomy but it did have an eerie, other-worldly atmosphere in the semi-darkness, and that, together with the smell of books, both new and old – because Greg sold antiquarian books as well as brand new ones – made her feel as if she had stepped back in time.

'Hi Tom,' she said. 'I'm sorry I couldn't do anything before but I'm so pleased Monday's good for us all. Anywhere in particular you'd like to meet. I'm happy to come to Folkestone. It's only a few minutes away.

'Hi Hope,' he said, and then laughed. 'Or should that be high hopes, because that's what I've got for our meeting. And I'm not talking about the business side of things, as I'm fairly sure you know. As for where to meet, we're both happy to go anywhere. What about at the hotel where I'm staying? It's got a great bar and an even better restaurant. Will you have time for dinner? Or is it just drinks? It'll be my treat if you do.'

Hope's heart was still reacting to the 'high hopes' comment, and it did a little dance when it caught up with the fact that both drinks and dinner were on the menu.

'I'm yours all evening.' Her seductive tone added impact to her words. His response sent a tsunami of desire crashing through her.

After a long and husky gasp, his voice was thick in his throat as he said, 'All evening, Hope?' putting extra emphasis on all three words.

They both knew it meant that breakfast was also on the menu if everything went well, and neither spoke for a moment as they each digested this fact.

Loud cheers and clapping from the back room of the bookshop returned Hope to the present.

'I wish I had more time to talk, Tom, I really do, but I'm at an event and I must get back. I'm sending you the sketch of the fairy grotto. I think it's perfect but let me know what you and Della think. Don't hesitate to say if you want any changes or have any suggestions. I'll be available to discuss it during the day tomorrow, although you might have to leave a message. Another hectic one I'm afraid. After that, I'm at an event in the evening from about five onwards till very late, and then the wedding on Saturday is an all day affair. But you can text or email me any thoughts or comments you or Della have and I'll get them dealt with. Sunday, I'll be around to talk, on and off, and then I'll see you on Monday.' Her voice caught in her throat at the thought of that. 'Oh! Where are you staying? It might help if I knew that.' She laughed.

'At the Trulove Folkestone Hotel. I chose it because Trulove Hotels are always excellent, but also because I thought it might be a good omen.'

'The perfect choice, Tom. Bye for now.'

She sucked in her breath and sighed wistfully. She wanted to dance and shout and throw all these books in the air. But Greg wouldn't be happy. And some of the books were beautiful, even she had to admit that.

She ran her hand gently along the spines of some older books and then spotted the locked bookcase containing red leather bound books with spines decorated and titled in gilt. They looked old. And expensive. You wouldn't keep ordinary books locked away. On closer inspection she saw that they were by J.R.R. Tolkien and a small note beside them stated that they were first editions.

She spun round on the spot and her eyes lit up as an idea struck her. But the clapping was slowing and she had to get back before the floor was thrown open for questions from the audience. She would need to speak to Greg in any case.

As she hurried to the back room her heart was pumping so hard that she thought she might pass out.

Could a person faint from too much excitement?

# Fourteen

Friday was hectic but Hope made time to call Tom with the good news.

'I think I've found the perfect venue for the proposal,' she said the moment he answered.

His laughter rang down the line. 'Good morning to you too, Hope.'

'Sorry, Tom. Good morning. What did you and Della think of the sketch, by the way?'

'That you were right. It's absolutely perfect. Della burst into tears so I know for certain she loved it. And now you've found a venue? You're incredible Hope.'

'Wait till I tell you what it is. It's a bookshop. And not just any old bookshop but one that stocks the largest selection of fantasy fiction books. They're Della and Alice's favourites, aren't they? The event won't be in the actual bookshop, but Della and Alice and their guests will be able to look around it. There's a large room at the rear and it's perfect. I spoke to Greg, the owner of the bookshop, last night and the room is free on Valentine's Day. He only really uses it for book related events and writing workshops and such, but he said he's happy to help on this occasion. I'll send you some photos of it before and during last night's event and then you'll get an idea of what can be done, bearing in mind that the fairy grotto will replace the murder scene.'

'Murder to romance. What a varied life you lead. It does sound perfect and if you think it is then I'm sure we'll think so too.'

'I do, Tom. We'll find someone to do the catering although Valentine's Day is a busy day for them so that may require us thinking outside the box, but we'll sort something out. We can provide trellis tables and decorate them beautifully to fit in with the whole fantasy fiction theme, and have a cold buffet. We also have a heated buffet bar if hot food is preferred, but again we'll need to see who'll be doing the catering first. Several caterers have their own. I have a friend who's going to open her own café soon and she's a brilliant cook. She doesn't have it yet but she can work out of our kitchen, or the one where she lives, or both. She lives near me and it won't be a problem to get the food to the venue. Della said she didn't want anything fancy. The horse and the fairy grotto were the most important things. There was a buffet last night as you'll see from the photos. Although we had a specialist caterer for that event, but you'll get the idea. After Alice says yes, which I assume is a sure bet, the party can continue until around eleven. There's even a large enough parking space at the rear for a horse box, so the horse can be unloaded there and Della can arrive on Brilliant Day without having to travel far at all. The life-size fairy grotto will sit perfectly along one wall of the room and we'll add plants, flowers, and some small blossom trees to fill any space on either side. There'll be a pool in the centre at the base of the backdrop, and the trompe l'oeil will have a waterfall cascading into it.'

'It sounds as if you've thought of everything.'

'It's my job to think of everything and that's why I'm paid the big bucks,' she laughed. 'But seriously, I hope I have. I want Della to have a truly magical day. And Alice of course.'

'I do too. I know it's your job, and I'll make sure I'm sitting down when I get your invoice, but I think you've gone above and beyond, Hope.'

'Thank you. If only I could find a real unicorn. And perhaps a fairy or two. But even I can't perform miracles.'

'Oh I don't know about that. I think you can. Ah. Sadly I'm the one who needs to go now. I've got an urgent call I must take. Have fun tonight and a wonderful wedding tomorrow.'

'Thanks. I'll call you as soon as I can.'

Hope sent the photos she had said she would, and then consulted her long list of things still to do, not just for Della's event but also for all the others in the diary of Eversley Events.

The rearranged meal for that night that Greg Carter's family had insisted must go ahead was the first one on that list. Eversley Events had taken over the organisation of the event because Naomi was now paying for it and she had asked them to do so.

But as Fiona's best friend, Hope was also a guest, as were Grace and Griff because Grace was best friends with Fiona's sister Naomi.

At events like these, where they were both the event planners and also guests, it was difficult but necessary to strike the right balance. But Hope and her family always managed it.

Hope made some calls to ensure she could tick the outstanding items from the list and then she moved on to the next one.

She repeated this process for the remainder of the day before she closed her laptop and went to her room to get ready for the evening ... and for her work.

Not that she or Grace did much work on the night. But they did do a lot of eating, laughing, singing, and dancing. It was more enjoyable than Hope had expected, and everyone had a wonderful time. The food was superb, the disco was good, and Hope pushed all her thoughts of Russell, and Laurence and Rob being in love with her to one side, although she did think about Tom once or twice. But he wasn't in love with her. Was he?

Drinking was kept to a minimum because Fiona's wedding was the following day, and Hope was Fiona's chief bridesmaid.

Hope had, of course, done most of the planning and implementation for everything in connection with the wedding, but as she had the important role of chief bridesmaid to perform on the day, the other members of the Eversley family would handle anything and everything pertaining to the event itself. Friends of Granny Joy would be taking care of her all day so they wouldn't need to worry about her, which was a blessing.

Luckily for all concerned the wedding went off without a hitch and even the weather was perfect.

It was one of the warmest February days on record and the sun shone from morning until evening. The bride looked sensational in a snow-white, off the shoulder, designer wedding dress of satin and lace exquisitely embellished with pearls making the dress both lustrous and glamorous, with a tiara fit for a Queen positioned regally atop a stylish updo with a scattering of tendrils at the sides. A necklace of a single row of pearls set with a diamante heart in the centre, and pearl and diamante heart earrings to match, made the most of the sweetheart neckline.

This was the first time Greg and his best man had worn top hats and tails, but no one would have guessed it. Greg was a tall and handsome fellow and he wore the outfit as if he had been born to do so.

The limousines were bedecked with white and yellow flowers, as was St Gabriel's Church. The ancient building looked resplendent and sunlight filtered through the stained glass windows casting rainbows of light dancing across the age-old tiled floor as the bride walked down the aisle.

The Reverend Brian Copeland performed the ceremony and as he had known Fiona and her family for many years, he ensured he gave his best.

The ceremony was followed by a four-course meal held at the same restaurant as the family gathering the night before, so it was back to Folkestone for the wedding reception and, once again, a disco that enabled revellers to show off their finest moves on the dance floor.

The honeymoon was two weeks in The Maldives which was a destination Fiona was more excited about than Greg, although this only became apparent when Fiona's sister Naomi, having won so much money on the Lottery, purchased tickets for them to take a once in a lifetime trip in a Grand Suite on the Venice-Simplon-Orient-Express to Venice, as a wedding present.

No one had ever seen Greg so elated. Not even on his wedding day. But Greg loved trains and couldn't get enough of them, which for a train driver, was really saying something.

That trip was booked for May but Greg was already talking about it more than he was his honeymoon. It didn't seem to bother Fiona who simply said that she was delighted to see him so happy.

'When your new husband is more excited about a train trip than he is your honeymoon, I think it's time to question your choice of life partner,' said Granny Joy when Hope and the others regaled her with tales of the wedding day.

But all things considered, it had been the perfect day and the perfect dream wedding.

# Fifteen

Rita and Vera Boot's eightieth birthday party was a far more raucous affair and resulted in the Reverend Brian Copeland appearing to be somewhat traumatised when he left, although his wife Daisy looked happier than anyone had seen her for years. They were both friends of Rita and Vera and had been invited as such, but the vicar had never been known to let his hair down.

Granny Joy said that the strippers were hot, which made Hope and Grace exchange looks as if they were about to vomit.

'I made fifty quid at the poker table. But some of that is now down the front of one particular pair of gold sparkly pants. And there wasn't much room, believe me.' Granny Joy chuckled.

'You weren't supposed to be playing with real money,' Hope exclaimed. 'I handed out the imitation notes myself.'

'I know you did,' said Granny Joy. 'We

decided we'd rather play for the real thing.'

'It's not illegal,' said Simon. 'Strictly speaking. Providing it's not a commercial enterprise.'

'Fabulous,' said Hope. 'No wonder the vicar was traumatised. Gambling and male strippers at the birthday party of two eighty-year-olds are enough to traumatise anyone who is expecting tea and crumpets.'

'I didn't know there were crumpets,' said Granny Joy. 'I haven't had crumpets for years. Your grandfather loved a nice crumpet slathered with butter.'

Hope rolled her eyes. 'I hope Bruce Boot doesn't phone us to complain. I dread to think what he must've thought about it all. Although he did know what they wanted. He was there when they requested it.'

'He has phoned,' said Pat, looking serious. And then she smiled. 'To give us a five star review which he says he'll be posting as soon as he gets home.'

'You haven't heard the best bit,' said Simon. 'We've already had five requests for birthday parties from, shall we say, the older generation.'

'I've only just brought Granny Joy home,' Hope said. 'They must have called as we were walking out the door. I did have a lot of requests for my card. Now I know why.'

Tom laughed when Hope told him all

about it later that evening. She had called him on the pretext of just checking he and Della didn't want any changes to the fairy grotto, and were happy with the venue for the proposal. They both knew that what was developing between them was more than a business relationship but for now Hope still needed to keep things vaguely professional.

'It sounds as if you had your hands full,' he said.

'I think those male strippers were the ones with their hands full. Their gold sparkly pants certainly were. And those ladies were rather liberal with their own hands.'

'You had fun though?'

Hope laughed. 'I did. Never judge a book by its cover, Tom. Those sisters look like butter wouldn't melt in their mouths, but they could set water on fire. They are lovely, and very sweet in a way, but I'm glad they're not my relatives. I don't think I've ever been so tired.'

'Then you'd better get some sleep. It's Monday tomorrow.'

Hope wasn't sure if he meant she'd better get some sleep because she was tired, or that she'd better get some sleep because she might not be getting much sleep tomorrow. Or maybe both. Whichever one he meant, his voice sent tingles up and down her body.

'You're right. And it's going to be another busy day. I'll see you and Della at seven in the bar of the Trulove Folkestone Hotel.'

'I'm counting the hours, Hope. Sleep well.'

'Me too, Tom. And you.'

She rolled over onto her back when she rang off. Who was she kidding? She wouldn't get much sleep tonight because all she would be thinking about was meeting Tom tomorrow.

Although when she did close her eyes, she had a vivid image of a tall, tanned man in a pair of sparkly gold pants with wads of ten pound notes stuffed down the front.

# Sixteen

Monday morning brought bitterly cold winds and torrential rain, but that was normal weather for February, so Hope didn't see it as a bad omen. She rather liked the wind and rain. There was something about a walk along the beach on a wet and windy day that made her feel even more alive than usual.

She wanted to look her best tonight, so she would not be walking anywhere if this weather kept up all day. Her dad had already offered to drop her at the grand entrance to the hotel, and the doormen would be on hand with giant sized umbrellas to hold above the heads of arriving guests until they were ushered out of the rain.

The weather was the least of her worries. Hope was feeling far more nervous than she ever had in her life and that very fact made her sure that there was something between her and Tom that was different from anything else she had experienced before.

She still didn't know what Tom looked like. She had been tempted to Google him to see if there were photos of him online, but for some reason she hadn't. Sometimes she did that with new clients and sometimes she didn't, and Tom was only supposed to be a client and nothing more.

Yet almost from the first time they talked, she knew that there was something different about him. That he had something no other client had. That made her less inclined to check him out – not more.

Hope might now have three men who believed they were in love with her but she hadn't had any real romance in her life for ages. Whatever this was with Tom felt very romantic from the off, almost as if it was meant to be, and she didn't want to shatter that illusion by searching for him online and seeing someone she didn't like the look of, or perhaps worse still, seeing someone she liked the look of far too much. She decided to let Fate take its course.

She hadn't asked Tom if he had looked her up. There weren't any photos of any of the members of Eversley Events on their website, just photos of some of the events they had organised. Pat and Simon had made the decision not to include photos of themselves or anyone who ever worked for them, especially Grace and Hope. There were some odd people in the world these days and women were especially vulnerable.

That was why Grace, Hope and even Pat never met a new client on their own unless they knew them beforehand, or they were a friend of someone the Eversleys knew. They always went in pairs or with Simon.

Meeting Tom was a risk but Hope had met Della in person on Christmas Eve, even if she hadn't been able to recall exactly what Della looked like, so as Tom was Della's brother, Hope felt safe with him. She was meeting him in a packed hotel bar, so she had a chance to get to know him before deciding whether or not to go anywhere else with him alone. A thought which once again sent tingles of excitement through her.

The day seemed to drag and Hope checked the time more than once or twice. A phone call from Rob that afternoon made her feel a little off balance. She hadn't seen him since the night he had kissed her on the beach and he was calling to say he wanted to meet up.

'We have things to discuss,' he said. 'I know it was a shock seeing me again like that but nothing's changed for me, Hope. I said the other day that I'd give you time, but I came home to be with you and I know, deep down, you want to be with me.'

'I don't know that, Rob. Eight years is a

long time. People change. We want different things now than we did back then. I'm not sure what I feel for you right now. That kiss was … nice, and it brought back memories of what we once had, but that was long ago and I'm not sure we can get that back. I'm not sure I want that back.'

'I can give you more time if you really feel you need it, but I want to see you Hope. I need to see you. Are you free tonight? We could go to The Royal Oak like we used to.'

'I'm not. I'm meeting someone for a drink. And dinner.'

'A man?'

'A client. But yes. A man.'

'But just a client?'

'I … I don't know.'

'What does that mean? How can you not know?'

'Because we … because I don't know, Rob. And you have no right to get cross. We are not together. We're not a couple. You may think you're still in love with me but I don't know how I feel about you.'

'What do you mean by that? I know I'm still in love with you. But you, it seems, are keeping your options open. Comparing us to one another. Is that it?'

'No. It's not. I'm simply getting on with my life. Which was what I had to do when you upped and left eight years ago. I'm not having this conversation, Rob. I told you I would think about what you said and I am. If you want to know how I feel right now I'll tell you. I think we ended eight years ago and now we're just friends. Whether we could ever be anything more again I don't know. What I do know is that I can't give you what you say you want at this moment in time. What you take from that is up to you. I must go. I have a lot to do.'

'So you keep saying. Don't keep me hanging, Hope. I won't wait around forever.'

'Then I think you have your answer. I waited for you for years. You've waited for me for, oh, less than one week.'

'Okay. I'll wait. I'll call you tomorrow.'

'No, Rob. I'll call you.'

Hope had hung up but the conversation left her with doubts. Was she doing the right thing by meeting Tom?

She had known Rob all her life – with the exception of the last eight years. They had a history together. Their parents were friends. They could build a life together in Betancourt Bay, assuming Rob meant what he had said about being home for good. They had been in love once. Could they be in love again? And would it last this time?

She knew nothing about Tom other than his voice turned her insides to goo and her heart raced every time they spoke. He lived hundreds of miles away. For them to have any sort of relationship meant she would have to move closer to him or he move closer to her. But Della and Alice had managed to have a relationship before Della moved to Folkestone to be with Alice.

Would Hope be prepared to move away? Her parents were upset about Grace moving across the road. Imagine how they would feel if Hope said she intended to move to Bournemouth.

She hadn't been prepared to travel the world with Rob. Not that he gave her that option. She could have tagged along perhaps, but he hadn't actually asked her to join him on his travels. She had always made it clear her intention was to return to Betancourt Bay after uni and work for the family business, Eversley Events so perhaps that was why Rob hadn't invited her to go with him. But when she asked if he planned to go alone, he had shrugged and said that it made sense, so she knew the answer was yes.

'This is something I need to do,' he had said when he'd first told her of his plans. Although he had clearly been planning it for a while and hadn't thought to tell her until a day before he left. When she had asked him why he had kept it a secret, he said that he knew if he told her she would ask him not to go and he had to do this for himself. He needed to get it out of his system.

Bournemouth was hardly the same as travelling the world, but it would still mean moving away from her family, her career, and the life she had always known.

Was that a bad thing though?

'Change is as good as a rest,' Granny Joy was often saying. Although Granny Joy frequently talked nonsense so putting store in anything she said might not be wise.

But Hope was jumping the gun. Moving to Bournemouth, or even having a real relationship with Tom might not be on the cards.

The one thing she hadn't thought about was that she and Tom might not like one another in the flesh. They might meet tonight and instantly hate each other. She doubted that very much but it was a possibility.

She spent the rest of the afternoon worried about what would happen if an even worse scenario came to pass. What if she liked Tom, but he did not like her? Or worse still from a business as well as a personal viewpoint. What if he liked her but she did not like him? After all the flirting she had done he would have a right to be a little ... cross. Della's event was still two days away. Could she keep up a pretence until that was over? As she had as good as said she would possibly be spending the night with him, that was a pretence too far. She had never slept with a man just for sex. To sleep with a man for her business, was a definite no-no.

By the time she got out of her dad's car that night, she was a nervous wreck. She had told her parents that she might be very late home, or possibly might be out all night. All she said was that she had a meeting in Folkestone that might run very late.

'I can come and get you,' Simon offered. 'I don't mind staying up.'

'No!' exclaimed Hope. 'I mean, no thanks. I'll sort myself out. I'll text you so that you don't have to worry and I'll see you at breakfast. Or maybe later if something comes up.'

The Trulove Folkestone Hotel was one of Folkestone's most prestigious hotels and the Trulove Hotel Group was known throughout the world for its culture of excellence. All the hotels had luxurious furnishings, first-class hospitality, and were beautifully designed. They had devoted hotel staff, the best chefs in the business, the finest wines, Michelin starred restaurants in many of the establishments, and most were situated in prime locations offering some of the world's finest vistas outside the grand entrances.

Portia Trulove now ran the hotel chain, together with her husband, Mikkel Meloy, and although they had made some changes since Portia took the helm, like making the hotels more eco-friendly, the same standards guests had come to expect from a five star, luxury hotel and spa, still held true. Portia's dad had handed over the reins earlier than most people expected, had gone off on a round the world cruise, and was now retired and enjoying life with his new wife. The seventh one, according to the online gossips. Hope didn't read those things but Granny Joy did, and Hope could remember her saying that there was another man she would have to cross off her list.

'You've got a list?' Hope had asked surprised by that.

'Of course I have. I'm not dead yet. I could still tango in the bedroom with the right man given half a chance.'

Hope had decided not to pursue the subject. Or to ask to see the list.

This hotel was near the Harbour Arm and offered superb views of the Harbour Arm, the white cliffs, and the English Channel, including Locke Isle.

But Hope was not interested in the view, or what the hotel had to offer. Tom was inside and this felt as if it might be the most important meeting of her life.

# Seventeen

The hotel bar was heaving with customers and Hope had no idea what Tom looked like, other than he was blond. And not as good looking as the actor Tom Hardy, according to Tom's own words.

But she did know what Della looked like. She might not be able to recall their entire conversation from Christmas Eve, but Della had certainly made an impression. Her hair was as white as the fake snow on the trees inside Betancourt and she wore it in a pixie cut. She had the brightest smile Hope had ever seen, especially on such an elfin-like face, and eyes that would outshine emeralds. She was tall and slim and very tactile.

Would Tom look the same?

It took less than a minute for Hope to spot him and he must have spotted her before she had seen him, because he was staring directly at her, his mouth slightly open, his eyes aglow and seemingly as green

157

and as beautiful as his sister's, his blond hair splashed with gold, gleaming under the lights above his head, his tanned face far more handsome than she could have hoped, and a smile on his generous mouth that sent electricity coursing through her. But when his gaze swept over her body taking her in from head to toe, she thought she must've burst into flames. And when she did the same to him, the heat grew more intense.

Had he experienced something similar as he had looked at her? The way his body seemed to tense suggested he had, and as they walked towards one another it was as if the crowd parted like the Red Sea.

It didn't of course. Hope had to squeeze her way through the throng of people and Tom had to do the same, but when they were finally face to face and they smiled at one another the cacophony around them faded into a distant, quiet hum and the only voice she heard was his.

'Hello, Hope,' he said huskily as his eyes met hers.

'Hello, Tom,' she replied, in her sexist voice.

'You're even more beautiful than I thought you would be,' he added, his voice thick in his throat as his eyes briefly took in her entire body once again, which sent new tingles and sensations to places she had forgotten existed.

She had checked in her coat (and her overnight bag having come prepared but not wanting Tom to know that) at the cloakroom in the hotel lobby and had removed the bolero top that went with the dress she was wearing, and slung it casually over one arm. She wanted to make the best impression and the tight-fitting bodice and slightly plunging neckline of the cashmere dress showed her cleavage to its best advantage with the jacket removed. But the soft fabric offered scant protection against the reaction of her body to Tom's close proximity, his seductive looks and his sexy voice. Perhaps the black lace, underwired bra was not her best choice? It left little to the imagination beneath the clingy dress

'Ditto,' she replied, making it obvious that she also appreciated what she saw.

His stunning smile grew wider and brighter, if that were possible.

'How did you know it was me?' he asked.

'I just knew,' she said. 'How did you know it was me?'

Again his all encompassing scan sent her body into overdrive.

'Ditto,' he said. 'Although I must confess that Della gave me a brief description. Long chestnut hair, hourglass figure, beautiful. Not much to go on. And she did you an injustice. Lustrous, chestnut hair, the perfect figure, breathtaking beauty, eyes that shine like sapphires and emeralds rolled into one, and lips that were made for kissing is how I would've described you. Briefly. I can go into more detail if you like.'

'Maybe later,' she said quivering at the thought of kissing Tom Hardy.

'Later,' he nodded, staring into her eyes. And then, with a slight shake of his head he smiled. 'Where are my manners? What would you like to drink?'

'A glass of white wine, please.'

He held out his arm to let her go before him and then somehow made space so they could walk to the bar side by side.

'Do you like champagne? This is a special occasion.'

'Doesn't everyone?'

He laughed as he caught the bartender's attention. 'Della doesn't particularly. But she drinks it on special occasions. Neither does Alice. They are so well suited it's as if they're twins. Although that would be weird so forget I said that.'

'Oh, where is Della by the way?' Hope scanned the crowd.

'Didn't I say?' He furrowed his brows and then gave his name and room number to the bartender. 'No, I didn't. I was so...' he coughed. 'Unfortunately Della won't be joining us. She sends her sincere apologies but Alice isn't well today and although it isn't anything to worry about, just a twenty-four hour tummy bug, they believe, Della felt she couldn't leave her.'

'I'm so sorry. You should've called and we could've rearranged.'

'I didn't know until about an hour ago. Della left it late to see if she might be able to get away, but she wants to ensure Alice is better for the big event on Wednesday, so thought it best if she stayed. I know I could've called then but ... being entirely selfish, I didn't want to. I wanted to meet you, Hope. In fact, I couldn't wait.'

The bartender reappeared with a silver ice bucket containing a bottle of Louis Roederer champagne, a brand that Hope knew was not the most expensive on the planet but certainly didn't come cheap. It was a popular choice and had ranked top of the list when Eversley Events had carried out a short survey amongst their most discerning clients.

Was Tom trying to impress her? Or did he simply like the brand? And, as he hadn't told the bartender what he wanted, had he already ordered this and had it put aside for tonight? The bartender placed three champagne saucers on the bar and Tom slid one back with a smile and his thanks.

'I ordered this before Della called,' he said, 'hence the three glasses. We prefer saucers to flutes but if you want a flute I can get one.' Hope shook her head. 'I hope you like it. I only drink champagne on special occasions but this is my favourite. Or we can ask for another brand if you prefer.'

All her questions having been answered Hope said, 'No. This one is perfect.'

'Shall we find a table?'

'I'm not sure there's one free.'

'It's certainly busy in here for a Monday night.'

'Perhaps it's early Valentine's celebrations,' said Hope.

'Perhaps.' He eyed her nervously. 'Please don't think I'd pre-planned this, because I haven't ... but...' he licked his lips hesitantly, ran a hand through his hair, and glanced towards the restaurant. 'Erm ... I ... I've booked a table for dinner but not until eight and ... erm...'

'Are you trying to suggest we take this to your room, Tom?' She stepped closer so that her body was touching his, and met his slightly startled yet excited look as his gaze shot back to her. 'Because if you are, I think it's a good idea.'

She saw him swallow hard and he nodded as if he couldn't speak.

'Shall I have this sent to your room, sir?'

the bartender asked as he reappeared from nowhere as if he had read their minds.

Tom nodded again, cleared his throat, and said, 'Yes please.'

A moment later he took Hope's hand in his and together they walked purposefully towards the lift.

# Eighteen

'This is without doubt my best Monday ever,' Tom said a few hours later, his voice still husky with desire despite the number of times they had already made love. Within five minutes of entering his room it was obvious to both of them that they wouldn't be going downstairs to dinner, and between heated kisses, and half removed clothing, Tom had breathlessly called to cancel the reservation.

'And mine,' replied Hope, looking deep into his eyes.

That was not a lie. Or even an exaggeration. Hope had never experienced anything like the hours she had just spent with Tom. There were no superlatives that could do justice to Tom's lovemaking skills. If she were comparing Tom with Rob – which she wasn't ... although in a way she was, Tom would win hands down.

And on the subject of hands, Tom had

done things with his that had made Hope feel sensations she had only read about in magazines. Satisfaction with Tom was guaranteed, over and over again. And again. And again.

'Are you hungry?' Tom asked, momentarily stopping his kisses along her shoulders, and gently and enticingly running his fingers down towards her stomach instead, as a clock chimed ten p.m. in the distance.

'Only for you,' she said.

He raised one brow. 'Again?'

She nodded slowly. 'Again. If you can.'

His smile was bewitching and breathtaking and filled with promise.

'Oh I can, Hope. And I want to. You have no idea how much.'

'If it's even half as much as I want you, believe me, I know.'

She wanted to scream out his name.

She wanted to make love with him all night and all day and the night and day after that.

She wanted to be with him for as long as she possibly could.

How long was that?

If she had her way it would be...

Forever.

She wanted to tell him she loved him.

Because she now knew that she did.

And it wasn't because he was handsome, or lovely, or funny, or fantastic in bed.

It was because it felt as if she was meant to be with him.

As if Fate had thrown them together because they fit perfectly with one another.

His voice made her heart sing.

His smile made it jump out of her chest and into his.

His touch made her body float in the air and react in ways she hadn't thought it could, or ever would.

His kisses made her melt but also feel as if she could take on the world and win no matter how hard the challenge it gave her.

With Tom by her side, she felt anything would be possible.

He laughed lovingly when, on asking her to stay the night, she told him she had left an overnight bag in the hotel cloakroom in the lobby.

'You came prepared?'

'I was ... hopeful, let's just say.'

'So was I,' he admitted. 'But when you walked into the bar, I knew you were way out of my league. I still had Hope though.'

Now she laughed. 'And having *had* Hope for several hours, do you still think I'm out of your league?'

'Absolutely.'

'I thought you were out of mine when I

saw you,' she said. 'And yet, it felt as if we were meant to be.'

He moved his head to look her in the eye. 'I felt that too. It was as if you and I were destined to meet. And as awful as this sounds, even Alice being ill and Della deciding not to join us, made it seem as if Fate was working in our favour.'

'Yes,' she said. 'And let's be honest. We were going to end up in bed together tonight whether Della was here or not.'

'Without a doubt.'

Hope texted her mum to say she wouldn't be home and was staying the night in town with a friend. She didn't mention a name and luckily in her reply, Pat didn't ask.

Tom called reception and had her belongings sent up, along with the food they both now desperately needed. Hope hadn't eaten since lunch, and all the exertion, as wonderful as it was, had depleted her reserves.

They ate until satiated, and then returned to one another's arms seemingly unable to satiate their passion for each other.

'I can't get enough of you, Hope,' Tom moaned softly, kissing her greedily and deeply.

'Ditto,' she whispered, matching his need. 'Double ditto. Oh God! Treble ditt-o-o-o!'

They finally fell asleep in each other's arms and awoke the next day as eager for one another as they had been the night before.

Hope spent as much of the day with him as she could, nipping back to his hotel room between meetings and popping in to see her family.

'Good night last night?' Pat queried when they sat at the kitchen table for a coffee and a chat.

Hope nearly choked.

'Better than I expected,' she said.

That wasn't a lie. She had expected it to be good but even her high hopes couldn't have imagined just how good.

Tom was waiting for her in the hotel lobby after Hope had texted she was on her way back to him and they ran hand in hand to the lift and tumbled on to the bed.

The next time she texted, he was waiting outside the grand entrance and almost tripped in his haste to get back inside.

'Next time I text, if you're already in here it might save a few precious minutes,' Hope suggested.

'I'll be waiting here in bed,' he joked.

'Hmm. That might give us a few more seconds. Instead of you having to get undressed, you could be helping me.'

He laughed and pulled her to him. 'You're a genius, Hope.'

'You bring out the best in me, Tom.'

She texted her mum to say she wouldn't be home that night and was staying with the same friend. Again, Pat did not ask who the friend was. Hope wasn't sure if she was relieved or not.

# Nineteen

'Will you be able to spend some of today with me?' Tom asked the following day.

'It's Valentine's Day, Tom.'

'I know it is.'

He produced a card, a bouquet of the most exquisite blooms with only one red rose in sight, much to her relief, and a bottle of the same champagne they'd drunk on their first night together.

'Two in one week!' she said, handing him the card and the voucher she had bought for him.

'For me?' He roared with laughter. 'I sounded like a girl then, didn't I? But I'm truly surprised. I've never had a Valentine's gift before.' It was a couple's, full body massage at the hotel spa, and Tom was clearly delighted. 'I was going to say all I want today is you, but now I get to have you and a massage with you. Wait. Did that sound wrong?'

'It sounded perfect. I'll see you at noon for the massage and then maybe we could come back here and have room service. I'll have to be at Bishop's Books this afternoon to set everything up for Della's proposal this evening, and the arrival of the horse, Brilliant Day, but I'll see you there later, yes?'

'Oh yes,' he said. 'I just pray Alice says yes too.'

'Do you think there's any chance she won't?'

'No. And now that she's fully recovered from that tummy bug, we know she won't be throwing up or dashing off to the loo.'

'You old romantic.' Hope rolled her eyes.

'Sorry. Too much information?'

Hope nodded and kissed him, and half an hour later than she should have, she left to go to The White House.

She couldn't believe her eyes when she walked into the kitchen.

'Wow! What are all these flowers doing here?'

'It's Valentine's Day,' said Granny Joy.

'I know,' said Hope. 'But Mum and Dad don't buy flowers for one another. Ah. Did Griff forget to tell the florist that Grace's address has changed? She'll be a bit annoyed.'

'They're not for Grace,' said Pat. 'They're for you. And I see you have some more.' She

171

nodded to the bouquet Hope held in her arms. 'Are those from your friend?' Pat grinned. 'They're beautiful. Give them to me and I'll put them in water.'

Hope was still trying to digest the fact that seven bouquets of red roses were for her. Surely Tom hadn't sent them? She had told him where she lived, mainly because they were discussing their lives and how they lived them. He told her he had a three-bedroomed house in Bournemouth; she told him she lived with her parents and had no intention of moving unless they threw her out.

'I love it there,' she said. 'Properties are hard to come by in Betancourt Bay. I've thought of moving to a flat in Folkestone like my best friend Fi did. But she moved in with her boyfriend. I don't really want to live on my own. I like coming home to a house full of people. And our dog.'

'I know how you feel. Della lived with me until she moved here to live with Alice last November. The house feels empty with just me. Perhaps I should get a dog? Or someone to share my home with?'

The look he gave her sent the joyful sound of bells ringing out in her head.

'Don't you want to know who they're from?' Pat asked.

'Yes,' said Hope, and she opened the

cards attached to the bouquets one by one.

The first was from Russell Betancourt and she sucked in a breath but when she read the handwritten note within the card, she smiled.

'I bought these to say I still love you, Hope. But I know now that you will never feel the same for me, and you were right when you said I should find someone who does. So these are for our friendship. Maybe next year, or the year after, or sometime in the future, I'll be sending roses to the true love of my life. I hope you find yours too. Love Russell xx'

The second was from Laurence Lake. The card read: 'To Hope. My inspiration. My muse. My friend. xx'

It seemed he'd thought about what she had said at his book launch and decided she was right.

The rest, to her great surprise, were from Rob Mills. Only one card contained a note.

'You know how I feel, Hope. Today is a busy day for you but I think we need to talk about us. Please meet me on the beach on Thursday, weather permitting. If it's raining, we'll meet somewhere else. I love you, Hope, and if you're honest with yourself I'm sure you'll realise you love me. I'll see you on Thursday. Text me and let me know what time is best for you. Love Rob.'

The fact that he hadn't added kisses irritated her for some reason. She grabbed her phone to call him and tell him he was wrong, but she thought better of it. He might've left her eight years ago but at least he did it face to face. She owed him that much. She would meet him on Thursday. And tell him she had fallen in love with someone else.

Because she had.

She definitely had.

She had fallen in love with Tom.

Yes it was fast. But did love have a time-frame?

People fell in love at first sight. She had fallen in love after their first conversation. Or maybe the second.

Perhaps she just liked him after the first.

If Rob asked her why, she wouldn't be able to tell him. She could only say that she did.

She texted Rob to thank him for the flowers and to confirm she would meet him on the beach the following day. It might be hard for Rob to hear her news but now that she knew how she felt, it was only fair that she told him. She wanted to tell the world. She wanted to shout it from the clifftop.

She loved Tom Hardy.

She adored Tom Hardy.

She wanted to be with Tom Hardy for the

rest of her life.

Because ... he had that special something.

She still had no idea what that was, but whatever it was, Tom Hardy had it in spades.

# Twenty

Della looked magical, especially as she sat astride Brilliant Day. They both seemed to glow beneath the lamplights in the mews at the rear of Bishop's Books, and the white cone shaped cardboard cut-out on the mare's forehead for the horn, secured in position with white ribbons and a white bridle, looked deceptively real. If Hope didn't know better, she would've believed in unicorns.

Della and Alice had already exchanged Valentine's Day cards, and Alice had given Della a gorgeous, silver heart shaped locket containing both their photos. Della was wearing it when she met Hope at the bookshop later that day.

But Della had told Alice that her present was in a bookshop and that she would meet Alice there at five-thirty that evening. She had lied and said that the shop shut at six so there was plenty of time to collect the gift.

Alice had naturally asked why Della

couldn't go and get it herself and hand it to Alice at home, and Della had explained that it was because Alice had a choice and could pick one of two things.

Della hoped that Alice would think it was a book – and in a way it was because Hope had arranged for a wooden box to be made to look like a book by one of Alice's favourite fantasy fiction authors.

Inside that book was another box. This contained the engagement ring that Della had had made. It was silver and was simple but beautiful, with the letter A inside the letter D, both entwined within the safety of twisted branches of a tree.

The plan was for Tom to arrive and lead Alice to the rear of the book shop where Della would be waiting outside in the Mews, seated on Brilliant Day. She would ride forward, dismount, and lead the 'unicorn' towards Alice. Della would take the book from the saddlebag and present it to Alice telling her that it could only be opened by a key and that key was inside the bookshop. Photos would be taken by a photographer, unbeknownst to Alice who would hopefully still be thinking this was all for her to get a book.

The couple would go inside where the six-foot high trompe l'oeil backdrop of the fairy grotto surrounded by fresh flowers, plants and several small blossom trees Hope had managed to source, would be revealed. All their family and friends would also be waiting there, Hope having let them all in when the couple were in the mews, before returning outside so that she could ensure Brilliant Day was safely ensconced in her horse box.

Alice realised that there was far more going on than her simply selecting a book, and burst into tears of joy, and everyone cheered. Alice and Della 'searched' for the key which didn't take long because Della knew it was hanging on a cherry blossom tree. Whilst Alice opened the box and the smaller box inside, Della got down on one knee and proposed.

Everyone cheered once more when Alice said, 'Yes.' And now, aware of the photographer's presence, Alice and Della posed so that more photos could be taken.

The champagne was opened but Della and Alice only drank one glass, followed by mocktails suitably embellished with cocktail sticks with little unicorns on top.

'That couldn't have gone better,' Tom said later, pulling Hope into his arms. 'It was worth every penny you're going to charge me.'

'I'm giving you our special friends and family discount,' Hope said, 'so it may not be quite as much as you expect.'

'Am I friend or family?' he asked. 'Because I know I've only just met you but you feel like family to me.'

'I think you've had too much champagne.'

He shook his head. 'It's not the champagne, Hope. But I will admit you make me feel light headed.'

And much later that night, or possibly in the early morning – Hope wasn't sure which because she had other things on her mind than checking the clock – Tom made her heart soar when he said the words she longed to say to him.

They had made love for the second time that night and were in that sleepy stage of bliss, satisfaction and sheer exhaustion. She was wrapped in his arms and she could feel his heart beating against her body.

'I love you, Hope,' he whispered.

'I love you too, Tom,' she whispered back.

His arm tightened around her and his soft gasp matched the one she had just made, but other than that, neither acknowledged the other's words and they drifted off to sleep, with Hope content in the knowledge that Tom Hardy loved her. Whether he had meant to say it aloud or not.

# Twenty-one

After Tom's declaration last night, and her own, Hope knew she had to speak to Rob. She had intended to meet him in any event but now it seemed more urgent. She took Lady E with her so that she didn't have to tell her parents that she was meeting Rob.

'You look different,' he said, as she let Lady E off her lead.

'Do I?'

She blushed because she felt different since she had slept with Tom. She felt stronger and more beautiful and more confident in some way.

'Yes. So ... have you given it some thought? Have you come to a decision?'

She nodded. 'I have, Rob.'

'And it is good news for me?'

She shook her head. 'Sadly not. Although in a way it is. I'm doing you a favour. I'm setting you free from whatever it is you think binds us together.'

'Love binds us together.'

'No it doesn't.'

'You've changed, Hope. And I'm not sure it's for the better.'

'Well I think it is. You can't come back after eight years apart and expect things to be just like they were when we were at university together. You made the choice to go travelling, not me. You were the one who wanted to go off and see the world in all its glory. And I don't blame you for that. Betancourt Bay wasn't enough for you then, how can you be sure it's enough for you now? It's always been enough for me.'

'I don't know, Hope. But my plan was always to come back to you. I told you that at the time. And as I said the other day, I just needed to get the wanderlust out of my system. I have. Holidays a few times a year will be enough for me now. I want to have a family, Hope. While I'm young enough to really enjoy them.'

'Life can't be all about what you want, Rob. I wanted things too. And I want things now. It's not the fact you went that broke my heart. It was because you just upped and left, telling me only the day before, and I never heard from you again. Until the other night. I don't want to be the one you come home to, Rob. I want to be the one you can't bear to leave. I want to be the prize. Not the consolation.'

'You are the prize. I've come back for you, Hope. You. Nothing else.'

'And you just expected me to be waiting for you.'

He shrugged. 'I wasn't sure. But my family kept me updated, so I knew you hadn't met anyone special. And I hoped you wouldn't. Until I could be sure that I could come back and stay. Doesn't the fact that you are still single tell you that you and I are meant to be together?'

'No. It tells me that I hadn't met the one for me. Until just recently.'

'The one for you? That's me, Hope. I'm the one for you, and you're the one for me.'

Hope shook her head slowly. 'No Rob. You're not. I thought you could be, once. But now I know I was wrong. I'm sorry Rob, but that's my final decision.'

He looked dejected and she felt sorry for him although there was no reason why she should.

She stepped towards him and squeezed his hand; he pulled her into his arms and hugged her.

She was going to push him away but he seemed to need this final hug and perhaps it wasn't such a bad thing.

Now they could at least part as friends.

# Twenty-two

'Did Tom Hardy find you darling?' Pat asked when Hope returned home half an hour later.

She and Rob had talked for a while after that hug and although he still maintained he loved her, Hope was certain it wouldn't take Rob long to get over it. He said he might as well do a bit more travelling.

'You never know. I might meet someone on my travels. Although I haven't so far.'

'You never know how or when you might meet the love of your life, Rob. I genuinely hope you do and I truly hope it's soon.'

'I'll send you a postcard and tell you,' he said.

'Just don't say I wish you were here,' she quipped.

They had walked back up the three hundred Lookout steps together with Lady E and had parted as friends with a final hug at Lookout Point.

'Tom?' Hope said now, an odd feeling itching at her skin. 'Was he looking for me? Did he call?'

'He was looking for you, yes. But he didn't call. He couldn't because you left your phone at Della's engagement party, last night. Or so he said. But I'm not sure I believe him.' Pat grinned. 'He came to the door about an hour ago. What a lovely young man he is. He apologised for calling round but said he thought you might need it.' She nodded towards Hope's phone, now recharging on the kitchen worktop charger. 'I told him you'd taken Lady E to the beach and how to get there via Lookout Point and the steps.'

'Oh God! When was this?'

Had he seen her with Rob?

'About ten minutes ago. Why? What's wrong Hope? You look as though you've seen a ghost.'

Hope grabbed her phone and called him but it went to voicemail so she left him a message. She tried to sound cheerful but her heart was thumping and not in a good way.

'Hi Tom. Mum told me you called round. Thanks for my phone. That was kind of you to bring it. I didn't notice I'd left it. I was on the beach with Lady E, our dog, and I bumped into an old friend. Erm. I'm home now so perhaps you would call me when you get this message. Bye for now.'

Pat eyed her thoughtfully. 'What friend? What's going on Hope?'

'Nothing. I'm fine. I need coffee. Do you want one?'

Hope counted the minutes and then the hours but Tom did not call back. She had now left him another two messages each one sounding less and less cheerful and light hearted to her own ears. She dare not call again or he would definitely think something had happened between her and Rob and that she felt guilty, if he had seen them hugging.

But what if something had happened to him? What if he'd had an accident and that was why he wasn't calling her back?

She phoned Della and put on a huge fake smile hoping it would reflect in her voice.

'Hi Della. Sorry to bother you but have you seen Tom?'

'Yes,' she said sounding less friendly than she had last night. 'He's gone back to Bournemouth. He's in the middle of negotiating a big deal and he got a call and had to go back. Or so he said. Why?'

'Back to Bournemouth! Oh. Erm. I just wanted a word with him. If you speak to him would you please ask him to call me? It is quite important. I've left him a message but I just want to be sure he knows I need to speak to him.'

'Okay. Is everything all right, Hope?

Between you and Tom, I mean. Because one minute he's telling me how great you are and how he might stay in Folkestone for longer than he'd planned and then today he comes bursting in here saying he's got to go back to Bournemouth and he doesn't know if or when he'll be coming back here. I thought you two might've hooked up, because you seemed to be getting on so well. Last night you looked like a couple. But when I asked him, he said it was nothing. And he wouldn't be seeing you again.'

'He … he said that? Those … those exact words? Nothing happened and he wouldn't be seeing me again.'

'Yeah. Even Alice was surprised. But Tom doesn't fall for people that often. In fact, I can't remember the last time he had a serious relationship. He's not a monk, don't get me wrong, but he's not the kind of guy who sleeps around. Anyway, I'll tell him you called. Bye Hope. Thanks again for last night. Alice and I are still buzzing.'

So that was it. Either Tom had seen her with Rob, jumped to conclusions and left in a fit of rage. Or she had just been a hook up, even though he didn't have many of those.

And yet. Last night he had definitely said he loved her.

She wasn't going to give up that easily. She kept ringing but each time it went to voicemail.

Finally she received a text.

'I'm back in Bournemouth, Hope. Business called and I had to return. Pretty busy so I can't talk right now. In constant meetings. Thanks for everything you did. And I do mean everything. It was a great hook up and we had a good time, didn't we? Take care, Hope. Send me your invoice and I'll pay it right away. Don't worry about the friends and family discount. We're not really friends, are we? And I don't believe in taking advantage of people. All the best. Tom.'

Hope's heart broke for the second time in her life.

But this time she was certain it would never mend.

Emily Harvale

# Twenty-three

Hope threw herself into her work but she wasn't really sure what day it was, where she was, or what she was doing.

She didn't really care either.

But there was one event she did care about and despite her heart being shattered into tiny pieces she was determined to put on a smile and do her best.

'I do trust you, Hope,' Griff said, 'but are you sure Grace will be happy about this? I'm certain she loves me and fairly certain she'll say yes, but she won't think it's too soon, will she? Or that I haven't made much of an effort by asking for your help?'

'Stop worrying, Griff. Grace adores you. Obviously I can't speak for her but I know my sister well, and she will love this. I've told you she wanted to propose to you herself on Valentine's Day, and if it wasn't for the fact you'd already asked me to do this, I would've let her go ahead. But again, I know Grace,

188

and she would rather you propose to her than for her to propose to you. That way she can be certain you don't have the slightest doubt about marrying her. And as you're proposing three days later than she had intended to propose to you, she can hardly think it's too soon, can she? As for asking for my help, she'll be thrilled. Firstly, because it means more money for the family business,' Hope winked, 'but mainly because it means you've gone to the trouble of making sure this proposal is special.'

Relief spread across his face and he breathed out a long sigh. 'Why am I so nervous? I think I need a drink. No. Not until Grace has said yes. I don't want to jinx it. What time is it?'

'It's two minutes after the last time you looked at your watch. Stop it, Griff. Everything will be fine. Okay, here she comes. Don't forget the ring is in your left pocket.'

Griff nodded. 'Left pocket. Left pocket. Okay. I can do this. Please say yes, Grace.' He marched to the double front doors and although the Great Hall was in darkness he knew precisely where the doorknobs were and he opened both doors just as Grace was about to get out her key.

'Thank you,' she said. 'I ... what's wrong, Griff? You look ... strange. And why is it so

189

dark in here? Has there been a power cut? I can hardly see a thing.'

'Thanks,' he croaked closing the doors behind her. 'You look more beautiful every time I see you.'

'You can hardly see me and I can only just see you. What's going on?'

He took her hands in his and pulled her close. But not too close. 'In fact you look so beautiful Grace, I don't think I'll be able to take my eyes off you all night. You outshine the stars.'

She gasped and her breath quickened as her chest rose and fell. 'Griff?'

'There's something I want to ask you,' he continued, looking her directly in the eyes. 'Dance with me?'

Her second gasp was louder, almost a little shriek, but it was joyful as the glow from hundreds of candles and myriad fairy lights strewn all around them, and from the massive chandelier in the centre, lit up the Great Hall.

The music started, provided by a string quartet from Folkestone, and a choir from St Gabriel's Church, just as it had been on the night of the Mistletoe Dance.

Now he did pull her close and she looked up into his eyes and beamed at him as they danced around the Great Hall.

'Those things you said. They were all the

things you said to me that night, weren't they? The night of the Mistletoe Dance. The night you told me you loved me.'

Griff nodded. 'If I remember correctly, yes. And the one thing I have is a good memory.'

'You've got a lot more than one good thing, Griff. You've got hundreds. Is this because we didn't really get to celebrate Valentine's Day properly? Wait. Did I just see Hope? What's she doing ... Oh. My. God!'

Grace almost crumpled in his arms but Griff held her tight. Only when he saw she was surefooted did he get down on one knee and take out the velvet ring box from his pocket.

Hope could see that Grace was shaking. With excitement and with happiness as her eyes filled with tears.

'I love you, Grace,' Griff said. 'I've always loved you. There has never been anyone else for me and there never will be. You made my dreams come true on Christmas Eve and you made me truly happy by agreeing to move in with me. Will you now make me deliriously so by saying you'll be my wife? I want to spend my life with you, Grace Eversley. I always have.'

'Yes!' Grace screamed. Screamed at the top of her lungs. 'Yes! Yes! Yes!'

Griff slipped the diamond solitaire ring

on her finger and wrapped his arms around her as he kissed her.

A kiss that lasted so long that Hope wasn't sure it would ever end.

When it eventually did, Pat, Simon, and Granny Joy, along with Lady E, and Archie, and Tabby the housekeeper, joined them in the Great Hall. As did Russell, whom Griff had called to ask to be here tonight.

'I wanted our families to join in with this celebration,' Griff said. 'I hope that's all right, Grace.'

'All right?' She looked at him with so much love in her eyes everyone could see it. 'I couldn't think of a more perfect proposal if I tried.'

Then Hope had the life-size painting by Hanna Shaw brought in from the morning room, and Grace and Griff gasped in unison as this was a surprise for them both.

'That's us!' Griff said his voice cracking with emotion.

'On Christmas Eve,' Grace said, crying with delight 'It's so beautiful.'

'You're beautiful,' he said. 'I meant it that night and I mean it tonight. You outshine the stars, Grace.'

'You're not so bad yourself,' Grace teased. 'And I love you with all my heart, Griff.'

Everyone waited until the couple had

finished kissing, and then Hope said, 'This is a gift from all of us in this room, and also from Hanna Shaw. Now shall we open the champagne?'

# Twenty-four

'Are you ready to talk about it now, Hope,' Pat asked the next day.

'Talk about what?' Hope was slumped in a chair at the kitchen table, drinking her umpteenth cup of coffee.

'Whatever it was that happened between you and that lovely young man, Tom Hardy. Or is that the problem? Did it turn out to be that he wasn't so lovely after all?'

'I don't know what you mean. He was just a client and that event is done.'

'Okay. That's enough!' Pat pulled out the chair opposite and glared at Hope. 'I'm your mother and I can tell when you're miserable and when you're ecstatic. When Tom Hardy was around you were ecstatic. And so was he the day he came here. Now he's gone and you're miserable. Who were you with on the beach that day, Hope? And more importantly why aren't you and Tom constantly calling one another anymore?'

There was no point in trying to hide it. Hope blurted it all out to her mum. The way she felt. The fact they'd slept together and how wonderful it was. She left out all the details of course. This was her mum after all. She told Pat about Russell and Laurence and Rob. She said what happened on the beach that day and what happened with Tom after that.

'The thing is, I really believed he loved me, Mum. But he didn't did he?'

Pat looked concerned and thoughtful.

'I think he did. And probably still does. I would bet he's as miserable as you are. If you had told me this sooner, we might not be having this conversation. Now I can't be certain but I think I'm right. You may want to talk to Barbra Brimble.'

'Barbra Brimble? Why would I want to talk to that gossip?'

'Precisely because she is a gossip. When I nipped out a few minutes after Tom left here that day. The day he brought your phone, I saw them both on the clifftop and they seemed to be having a deep conversation.'

'Tom and Barbra? On the clifftop at Lookout Point?'

'Yes darling. As I said, I may be wrong but I believe that whatever is happening between you and Tom now may have

195

something to do with bloody Barbra Brimble.'

Hope grabbed her phone and dashed to the front door yelling, 'I'm going to see Barbra, Mum. I won't be long.'

Less than a minute later she was knocking on the door of the Brimble's bed and breakfast.

'Oh hello dear. How lovely to see you. Do come in.'

'Hello Mrs. Brimble. I can't stop but I need to ask you a question. Do you recall chatting with someone on the clifftop last Thursday? At Lookout Point. A young man about my age. Blond hair, good looking, tanned.'

'Why yes! Such a handsome young man. I thought he was thinking of jumping at first. People do you know. Times are hard these days and some people think it's their only option. But it doesn't solve anything, does it? Or I suppose it does for them but not for those they leave behind.'

'What? You thought he was contemplating suicide?'

'Yes. But he said he wasn't.'

Hope asked her to describe him just to be certain, and it was definitely Tom.

'This is really important so please think carefully. Can you remember what you said to him or what he said to you?'

'Well this is a strange request. I'm not one to repeat conversations.'

'Please! It means the world to me. I need to know what happened that day. It might not change anything but then again it might change everything.'

'Well I'll try. Now let me see. I thought he was going to jump and he said he wasn't, and then ... oh I know. Yes of course. I saw you and Rob on the beach below and do you know what? I think he might've been watching you. How odd is that? But I think he was here on holiday because I've never seen him before. I hope I didn't put my foot in it. I thought you and Rob were back together but I've heard you broke up with him. And there was me telling that lovely man how wonderful it was to see you two back together. I don't gossip but I was so pleased and I think I told him more than I should. I believe I said how much in love you two were. He did look surprised, now I think of it. I told him you'd been sweethearts all your lives, that you went to university together, but that the silly boy went off travelling and left you here waiting for him to return. And how there you both were still in love after all these years. But how it was important to you youngsters these days to sow your wild oats before you settled down.'

Hope had listened in disbelief. How

could the stupid woman have said all that? And to someone she thought was a stranger.

Now Hope knew what had happened. Tom thought she'd lied and that's why he'd left without saying goodbye.

But was it also why he'd texted those things to her about it only being a hook-up? Or had he meant that?

No. Even her mum was sure Tom cared for her.

He had seen her and Rob and believed what Barbra Brimble had told him. If he saw them hugging that would only have confirmed it. Is that why he went back to Bournemouth?

'Thank you so much Mrs Brimble.'

'I hope I've helped.'

'You have.' Hope was about to leave but she stopped and looked directly at Barbra. 'But the thing is Mrs Brimble, it would've been a lot more helpful if you hadn't told someone you thought was a stranger all those things in the first place. Perhaps, in future, you might try minding your own business and not someone else's. Goodbye.'

She called Tom right away and when she got his voicemail yet again she left him a message.

'I know what happened Tom and it's not true. The man you saw me with that day was my ex-boyfriend from eight years ago. He wanted me back and I said no. I haven't been waiting for him. I'm not in love with him. We parted that day on the beach as friends. I don't know how you feel about me now, and if you meant what you said about it just being a hook up that's fair enough. But I don't think you did. I think you felt hurt and betrayed because you think I lied to you. I didn't lie to you, Tom. I'll never lie to you. Barbra Brimble, the woman you talked to that day on the clifftop is a silly and sometimes nasty gossip. Nothing she said was true. Apart from that Rob and I once dated. And we did go to uni together. Oh, and he did go travelling and I came home. But I was always coming home whether Rob did or not. I don't love him, Tom. I love you. If you don't feel the same, I'll understand and I promise I won't bother you again. At least I'll try not to. No. I'll do better than try because I know what it's like to have people chasing after you when you don't feel for them what they feel for you. So this is the last time I'll call you. Unless you call me back. That's not an ultimatum. It's me saying I truly hope you'll call me and give me a chance to explain. I won't lie. I don't do that. And I'll answer any questions you may have. Just call me, please, Tom. Call me! I really hope you do because I think we have something. That special something that everyone is searching for. At least that's how I feel. I love you Tom, with all my heart. All I need to know now is, do you love me? I hope the answer is yes.'

Hope could do no more than she'd done. She couldn't jump in the car and drive to Bournemouth. Tom might not love her and she couldn't make him.

Just like Russell Betancourt couldn't make her love him.

Tom had her phone number and he knew where she was.

Now she had to hope that Tom Hardy thought Hope also had that special something. And that he wanted to see her again.

# Twenty-five

Every time her phone rang, Hope's heart leapt to her mouth, but each time it hadn't been Tom calling.

Hope took Lady E to the beach to try to clear her head. It had been an entire day now since she had left him that message and she had heard nothing from Tom. Not even a text to say he'd meant it about the hook up.

But then again, not hearing from him was probably an answer itself. If he felt for her what she felt for him he would've called her back and told her.

The beach was beautiful tonight, as it always was. Or nearly always. The moon was full and it lit up the sand like a stage. This was obviously a one-woman show and it always would be now. Well, one woman and the family dog.

She was later tonight and she thought she would be here alone at almost midnight, but she had seen a couple holding hands and another person walking their dog. And now there was someone running. At this time of night. Blimey. He must be dedicated.

Oh no. Not him. Hope couldn't deal with him tonight. She thought Rob had left already, but there he was running along the shore in the moonlight. His blond hair and his tanned body glistening as if he was in the spotlight. The last thing she wanted was Rob feeling sorry for her because it had no doubt got around that Tom had been on the cliff that day and he'd seen her and Rob together. Barbra Brimble would make sure everyone knew. Hope would try to ignore him.

Lady E had other ideas. She ran towards him and did her little dance. The same one she had done the first night she saw him. But then again, that crazy little dog did that dance for everyone. She just wanted as much attention as she could get. And who could blame her?

He stopped, bent down, and petted Lady E and then he looked up and scanned the beach turning his head until he saw Hope. Now she couldn't avoid him.

She could see, as he got closer, that he looked a bit different tonight. Remarkably different, the closer he got.

And that was because...

It wasn't Rob!

Hope held her breath for so long it was a

miracle she didn't pass out.

Tom Hardy stopped right in front of her, his breathing rapid and his chest rising and falling as he looked at her.

And then the broadest smile swept over his face and his eyes shone with love and desire.

'Hello Hope,' he said.

'Hello Tom,' she replied.

He stepped closer and his eyes scanned her body. 'You look beautiful.'

She scanned his. 'So do you. Did you get my message?'

He nodded slowly. 'Loud and clear. I drove here as fast as I could, but as it was so late, I thought I'd better wait until tomorrow.'

'Why didn't you return my call?'

'Because I wanted to say what I have to say in person. And because despite what you said I thought you might hang up. Or not take my call. Because there are some jerks who do that.' He was pointing at himself. 'Can you forgive me for believing the things that woman said? And for seeing two people hugging and assuming the worst.'

She nodded. 'Absolutely. I think, if I'm honest, I would've believed it too if I was in your shoes.'

'I should've realised it might not be what I thought it was. I should've stayed and asked you. Especially after you had said you loved me the night before, and I had said I loved you. And I do love you, Hope. I really do. You've got that special something that I've been looking for my entire life.'

'Ditto,' she said.

'There's just one tiny problem. I live in Bournemouth and you live here.'

'I'm willing to come to Bournemouth at some stage, if you're asking.'

He shook his head, 'I'm not.'

Her heart missed a beat.

'No of course. It's too soon to think about that.'

He raised his brows. 'Too soon? Is it? Only, I think it makes sense for me to come to you. I can't bear the thought of being so far away from you again. I drove like a madman and it still took me ages to get here. What do you feel about me finding somewhere to live in Folkestone? My tools are sold in stores but mainly online so I can live almost anywhere. Your family are in Betancourt Bay just a mile or so from my sister and her fiancée, so it makes sense for me to come to Folkestone.'

'I ... I think that's the best news I've heard all day. Well, not the best news. The best news is that you love me.'

'I do, Hope. More than you can imagine.'

'Oh I don't know. I can imagine a lot.' She stepped closer so that their bodies were touching and he slid one arm around her waist 'Are you staying in the same hotel? Because if you are I have an idea.'

He nodded. 'I like where this is headed.'

'I just have to take Lady E home first, and then I can join you at the hotel.'

He shook his head. 'Nope. I'm coming with you and I'll wait outside while you grab what you need, because if you think I'm letting you out of my sight tonight, you're wrong. And I might try to persuade you to stay all day Monday too. Because Monday recently became my favourite day of the week. Although if you're by my side, every day will become my favourite.'

'Ditto,' she said. 'Now please kiss me.'

'Anything you say.'

He held her tight and kissed her deeply and passionately and she kissed him back with the same intensity.

She still didn't know was that special something was but whatever it was Tom Hardy had it in spades, and it seemed Tom thought the same about her.

# Coming soon

Visit www.emilyharvale.com to
see what's coming next.

Plus, sign up for Emily's newsletter, or
join her Facebook group, for all the latest
news about her books.

Stay in touch with

# Emily Harvale

If you want to be the first to hear Emily's news, find out about book releases, see covers and maybe chat with other fans, there are a few options for you:

## visit: www.emilyharvale.com

Or join her Facebook group for all of the above and to chat with others about her books:

www.emilyharvale.com/FacebookGroup

Alternatively, just come and say 'Hello' on social media:

 @EmilyHarvaleWriter

 @EmilyHarvale

 @EmilyHarvale

# A Note from Emily

Thank you for reading this book. I really hope it brought a smile to your face. If so, I'd love it if you'd leave a short review on Amazon, or even just a rating.
And, maybe, tell your friends, or mention it on social media.

A little piece of my heart goes into all my books. I can't wait to bring you more stories that I hope will capture your heart, mind and imagination, allowing you to escape into a world of romance in some enticingly beautiful settings.

To see my books, or to sign up for my newsletter, please visit my website. The link is on the previous page.

I love chatting to readers, so pop over to Facebook or Instagram and say, 'Hello'. Or better yet, there's my lovely Facebook group for the latest book news, chats and general book-related fun. Again, you'll find details on the previous page.

# Also by Emily Harvale

The Golf Widows' Club
Sailing Solo
Carole Singer's Christmas
Christmas Wishes
A Slippery Slope
The Perfect Christmas Plan
Be Mine
It Takes Two
Bells and Bows on Mistletoe Row

**Lizzie Marshall series:**
Highland Fling – book 1
Lizzie Marshall's Wedding – book 2

**Goldebury Bay series**:
Ninety Days of Summer – book 1
Ninety Steps to Summerhill – book 2
Ninety Days to Christmas – book 3

**Hideaway Down series**:
A Christmas Hideaway – book 1
Catch A Falling Star – book 2
Walking on Sunshine – book 3
Dancing in the Rain – book 4

**Hall's Cross series**
Deck the Halls – book 1
The Starlight Ball – book 2

**Michaelmas Bay series**
Christmas Secrets in Snowflake Cove – book 1
Blame it on the Moonlight – book 2

## Lily Pond Lane series
The Cottage on Lily Pond Lane – four-part serial
Part One – New beginnings
Part Two – Summer secrets
Part Three – Autumn leaves
Part Four – Trick or treat
Christmas on Lily Pond Lane
Return to Lily Pond Lane
A Wedding on Lily Pond Lane
Secret Wishes and Summer Kisses on Lily Pond Lane

## Wyntersleap series
Christmas at Wynter House – Book 1
New Beginnings at Wynter House – Book 2
A Wedding at Wynter House – Book 3
Love is in the Air – spin off

## Merriment Bay series
Coming Home to Merriment Bay – Book 1
(four-part serial)
Part One – A Reunion
Part Two – Sparks Fly
Part Three – Christmas
Part Four – Starry Skies
Chasing Moonbeams in Merriment Bay – Book 2
Wedding Bells in Merriment Bay – Book 3

## Seahorse Harbour series
Summer at my Sister's – book 1
Christmas at Aunt Elsie's – book 2
Just for Christmas – book 3
Tasty Treats at Seahorse Bites Café – book 4
Dreams and Schemes at The Seahorse Inn – book 5
Weddings and Reunions in Seahorse Harbour – book 6

## Clementine Cove series
Christmas at Clementine Cove – book 1
Broken Hearts and Fresh Starts at Cove Café – book 2

Friendships Blossom in Clementine Cove – book 3

## Norman Landing series
Saving Christmas – book 1
A not so secret Winter Wedding – book 2
Sunsets and Surprises at Seascape Café – book 3
A Date at the end of The Pier – book 4

## Locke Isle series
A Summer Escape – book 1
Christmas on Locke Isle – book 2

## Betancourt Bay series
That Mistletoe Moment – book 1
That Winter Night – book 2
That Special Something – book 3

To see a complete list of my books, or to sign up for my newsletter, go to
www.emilyharvale.com/books

There's also an exclusive Facebook group for fans of my books.
www.emilyharvale.com/FacebookGroup

Or scan the QR code below to see all my books on Amazon.

Printed in Great Britain
by Amazon